Cover by Brosebookcoverdesignz

To those who like their men with a little bite...

DEDICATION.

I have run out of people to dedicate my books to sadly.

So, this is for all the ladies out there (and the men of course) who rather like the bad boys.

Rhys is as bad as it gets.

A bad daddy vamp.

TRIGGER WARNINGS

This book contains an unhinged, ruggedly handsome long haired rugged vampire, who will do all matters of unspeakable things to those that fuck him off in any shape or form, and he will also always defend his fated mates' honour in any way that he can do so.

There is a conversation between two vampires discussing how they became vampires, that may trigger some.

May contain random cussing, violence, and some not-so-sweet loving by his truly as he takes what he believes is owed to him.

His long-awaited fated mate.

RECAP FROM BOOK ONE

In the last book, it was revealed that Iden the vampire had a human-fated mate living in the great, old city of Norwich. His friend who he had saved from coming to harm and turned her into a vampire just like him to save her dear life, told him of this fact.

It seemed to be that little old Ruby could find the human mates by their scent and their scent alone, which to her smelled exactly like their vampire mate did.

It also turned out that Ruby's beloved sister was Iden`s human mate.

Once they were thankfully acquainted, Iden choked his mate to death during sex as she asked him to, so that she could be with him in the hidden vampire realm and see her sister whom she had not seen in five years due to her being a vampire which she had just found out.

And of course – her sister Ruby was invisible.

Elfina badly wanted to be with her sister again but Rhys, Iden's crazy brother had just gone and kidnapped her, sweeping her off to the dark side of the realm. During an unwelcome visit, he had been strangely drawn to Ruby that he became full of rage and longing and so he thought she was possibly his long-awaited destined mate.

When she clearly wasn't.

It was only later that very day after he arrived back at his castle that he lost his temper with her and found out that she was only into girls, that he realised his unfortunate blunder and cursed himself internally.

Likely externally too.

HIS INVISIBLE HATE

BOOK TWO.

Then

He hovered in mid-air, the hum of his huge, black bat wings beating against the chilling air. He as he arrived, peered down at the cliff edge to shockingly find his own blood brother lying motionless on the rocky ground below.

Well nearly below.

It appeared that he hadn't reached where he had intended to go to.

His body was twisted at a point unnaturally, and it was completely obvious from the severity of the angle that his limbs had been broken by the force of the fall off of the harsh cliff.

Tears stung the mighty powerful vamp's eyes as he silently descended down to the cliff, carefully folding his wings behind him as he landed softly next to the

7

crumpled figure so that his wings were safe from any falling rocks or sharp edges that might pierce them.

Hoping beyond hope that everything would pan out all right once he reached the other male.

Anger and regret roiled inside of him as he beheld the broken body of his beloved brother in his sights. His reckless one.

Iden.

He had it appeared to have thrown himself recklessly into an abyss of darkness due to a sudden fit of despair.

He had known, after all the times that he had watched over his little brother while he was living among the dead, that his brother's mental state had been deteriorating for some time. Yet he hadn't expected it to sink so low as to cause him to fling himself off something without considering the consequences of what would happen if he didn't make it.

Or if he did.

Or perhaps he had.

"Iden, Iden wake up!" Rhys shouted frantically as he shook his sibling's shoulder, feeling the lifelessness of their body. His eyes were wet with tears and panic as he looked out to see the cliff in front of him, remembering the sound of his brother's screams before his body had gone limp after falling from the dizzying heights.

He stayed motionless for a moment, still hoping that maybe there was a chance his brother might survive. But when no response came and there was only an eerie silence, he knew that all was likely now lost.

Unless he was flung off that cold, hard cliff. Then this was no accident.

Did he expect a miracle to arise? Because that was what it would take to save him right then after the metres he had fallen onto his doom.

But Rhys luckily for his brother- had plan B.

Backup plan.

For he was a vampire, that was the plan B that he had come up with. If he hurried, then he could bring his brother back when he soon passed for his next journey onwards – for all of eternity. Would he thank him for it?

Probably not.

"Iden, I said wake up." He yelled loudly into his still brother's curved ear. The ear barely twitched but something was going on still there. He sighed.

A gasping sound, then a groaning shuddering whisper,

"Just leave me here to die. It is all I deserve. All I want. All I needed." His brother sighed also, but he clearly was in agonising pain from the half assed fall.

Soon he would be gone from that world. Then there would be nothing left of his body but scraps for the wild animals to gnaw on that were lingering, watching, and waiting for their next meal. They would climb that cliff as soon as he had breathed his last breath and dig in hungrily.

Maybe even before.

"I can`t do that." His older brother raged at him crossly. Wanting to shake him again and again. Not even keeping his temper in his brother's near moment of his own death.

As usual.

"Rhys is that you?" Iden asked him quietly. The human one then grew eerily quiet. Either dead or listening out for a reply to his strange question. A weird one because his brother was dead.

Wasn't he? But there was shockingly for Iden a reply.

"Aye," Rhys said simply.

"Where are you?" The crumpled one looked around with one startling blue eye open and the other shut firmly sealed tight as if to keep his demons away and from ever appearing again. "Where am I now?"

"I am here. You are there. It is complicated but you cannot see me. You will see me soon; I promise you that." Rhys soothed with his raspy voice. "But don't worry I am still as overly handsome and witty as the last time that we both spoke my younger, stupider sibling. In fact, in the time that we were apart I have grown more so."

Not really the right time to smile but he did it anyway.

"The first bit maybe because it runs in the family. The second part was a firm, hard no. Not in this world or the next will you ever be named as witty brother," Iden muttered under his dying breath.

His brother smirked as he picked the words up with his sharp supernatural hearing.

Rhys said, "But I am invisible to your eyes so how do you know otherwise?"

A good, honest question.

"I think I am possibly hallucinating now," Iden said to him shakily. "The bang to my head must have done that," A former shadow of his usual self. "You can`t be here. You are gone. Long gone. Dead as a deceased dodo."

"Brother I am here. I didn't die that day that I left the family, the day I went missing... whatever you think happened to me didn't. Instead, I became...I became a vampire."

He heard his younger stubborn brother let out a pained laugh which was all he expected in his current pained condition, "Look it sounds crazy, but it's true. Let me turn you and then you can live with me... forever. Then this all won't matter anymore. Whatever it is, this thing you are going through now, the thing that made you jump from this cliff..."

Rhys urgently ran his hand over his brother as he could smell that his time was getting incredibly near, as to give him a hint of his own power to keep him going all the moment longer.

But not long enough.

"The jump was exhilarating. I have to admit. I would do it again if I wasn't already half dead from the first time." Iden declared. His brain obviously doing better than his battered body was.

"Luckily you had me to catch you before you tumbled down any further then brother. Wasn't it?"

The power that Rhys gave the battered Iden, would give them a bit longer to talk, but not long enough if Iden kept stupidly arguing with him and didn't believe in what he had to say to him.

His truth.

Stubbornness ran in the family as well as good looks it so seemed. Now it was beginning to show itself from the back to the front.

Iden said the words aloud that he had wanted to speak for so long but had never had the courage to, "I wanted to die."

"I know."

"I wanted to die and that is why I am here on this sodding cliff in the brambles that encase it. Leave me, the voice of my brother that left us all for good. Leave me, for I know my sins for I have earnt them." Iden shifted on the ground but moved barely an inch for he was stuck tight.

Broken and in agony.

It was all that he could muster from his fall down the rocky cliff.

"Just wished that I could have made it further down somehow. Darn bloody thorn bush! Darn gone wrong suicide! I couldn't even do that right could I!"

He tried to move away from his brother's forceful grip if it really were his brother that was, for he was still not sure, but he still remained a firm grip on his right arm and held it there in his clutch.

"Yes, that you did. That you did... But now you can live. Let me help you. Please." Rhys insisted of him. "You were bad at most things in life we both know that if we are being honest. You can try again in your second chance to be the man that you should have been..."

"This isn't true, this isn't true..." Iden muttered over and over again until the words stuck on his long, thick swollen tongue. It hurt and he feared that he had bitten it on the way down. The fall that he had not expected to survive. "I am dead. I can now hear my dead brother speak to me. Feel his hold even though he is not there in person to touch me, comfort me or to help."

"Oh, it is true youngest one." A pause. "Now do you want to live? Or should I leave you here to die alone?" A breath that Iden couldn't see hit his face.

Maybe Rhys was there?

He could smell him. Hear him. Feel him. But was it really his brother or did it mean that the end was nigh for him and his time now firmly up?

"You have to believe me; I didn't want to live but I also didn't want to die either… I wasn't sure what I wanted I tell you. No, I made my choice this is it and I will stand by it." Iden was still arguing but now with himself as he surely had done many times before the long, rocky cliff fall.

Rhys was beginning to wish that he had thrown his brother down the cliff rather than he himself had. If he had done there would have been no mistakes and he would not have lived this long in time to argue with him over pointless things. "I am going to turn you. It is the only way." He said.

"Turn me. What the hell!"

"Turn you." His big brother repeated as though Iden were simple.

Was his younger brother thick as well as battered and edging towards his death?

"Let me think. Please." Iden was then scarily still as he pondered.

Was he thinking, or busy dying? His brother did not know. But at the moment he did care.

He did not reply, and his elder brother was beginning to worry that he had maybe sadly passed or was to soon be. He hadn't sensed the passing of his sibling's soul goes past his own one, but he guessed that it was much different when the soul you had to collect was your own kin.

Emotions kicked in.

Mistakes could be made...For forces were at work there.

Had he missed it, him passing him through into the sky? That would be a first for him indeed Rhys boastfully thought.

But then Iden spoke out.

He said in a quiet reply in a gravelly voice, "No. The answer is no. If you are my brother, then something brought you back that shouldn't have... Leave me to die and relish in my victorious suicide. Let me do something right for once. Please let me at least have that."

The next thing that happened was Iden began screaming a terrible blood-wailing scream as his god-forsaken brother he hadn't thought still lived brought him to his actual death. He hadn't listened to his plea to die for good, his plea just to die right there and then.

Instead, he just took his brother's delicious crimson offering and took it for his own.

Then before his brother passed, he gave him his in return.

And the choice has been made.

Well, kind of

CHAPTER ONE

Now

RHYS

The next morning once Sniggles was back in his owner's reach, Iden and Elfina trundled through towards the darkness aimlessly, Iden taking the lead and Elfina struggling to keep up what with being a newly developing vamp, the oh-so-dark one - Rhys sat on a makeshift throne in his glorious castle that was his fucking sanctuary.

He loved it there.

Surrounded by fire and blazing lava that burned, his castle was in front of a real-life manic volcano.

Trendy.

Dragons flew high in the dark swirly air, and crazed unicorns like something out of a depressed child`s imagination shrieked in what was left of the trees that were then there.

Nothing was nice there in that part of their world. But still, some wanted to stay there and live nearby. Some wanted the thrill of bad rather than the quenching release of doing good for one another.

The sunshine was nearly gone in the sky – replaced with something else entirely…darkness.

"They are coming for me," Ruby said with a scowl at the tall, dark horrible vamp that sat upright on his throne with no slump to his person.

She wore a black, stunning dress that she had been made to wear that she hated more than this guy who had imprisoned her there. It matched the black suit and trainers that he donned.

Luckily for her, he had not actually touched her in any way since he had first tried on her first day there, as she did not think she would be able to handle a guy touching her like that again after her disgusting attack from five years ago.

It made her stomach crawl to think of being penetrated, even just touched, and she guessed that Rhys was fully aware of that for he had not tried since. And he seemed the sort that was a bit of a goer from all the sexual innuendo jokes he made.

Not funny ones.

"I know." Rhys grinned evilly with a twist of thin lips. "I'm counting on it!" He was so darn bad, Ruby thought that if he smiled with happiness even now and again he could look somewhat handsome to some. But the whole bad thing, bad boy act he had going on with trying too hard to be bad all the time was dragging his looks down in her simple opinion.

Her neutral one.

"You must know by now that I am not, she who you have been searching for." She explained quietly. Meaning his oh-fated one that she really wasn't.

He eyed her with a roll of the dark soulless eyes. "I...I am beginning to see that now my pretty. But why did you smell of her then back when?" His dark eyes with a trace of red burned deep into hers at the remembrance of the delicious smell that had invaded his senses a few days prior when he had busted in on his brother.

And found oh so much more.

He flexed his clawed fingers, and she sighed in annoyance and possibly boredom with that. Because they had been over and over the same thing like a stuck record since she had been brought there and kept prisoner by his great, dark lordship.

One everyone feared.

And sometimes her head fogged over, and her thoughts became…dark. She could only guess what the darkness had done to this vicious man in front of her over the years was what it was trying to do to her.

Many people would have gone mad, unhinged, with the insanity of it all! But she was now strong. Strong as come be.

She had had to have been.

"I don't know." She muttered quietly over and over.

For she did not. And she was beginning to worry that she would be penalised for not doing her work, although this male there had said he had temporarily sorted it with the judgers.

Had he though?

He could find his mate and live evilly ever after, and she could be banished or put down even for not doing her soul work in her absence. Which was a bit difficult when she was locked in some eerie fucking castle and only given blood now and again when he remembered that she was also a bloodsucker like him!

Rhys growled, "Well then you will be here for a long time my pretty. Let's hope the darkness doesn't take you before my brother tries to." He winked.

But to him the darkness was great. He did not see everyone's problem with it. If he could have his own way then the whole realm would be shrouded in it.

"He will kill you before that happens! He and my sister. His fated mate." Ruby said. She gasped in realisation as Rhys spun around in a fierce whirlwind. The shadows that often lingered in the room followed him everywhere that he went now as if he was their daddy.

Did they follow him out of the realm she had wondered, or did they stay in there impatiently waiting for him to arrive?

Rhys held his chin in deep thought and mused like the villain he was, "His mate? Hmm. That is new. I wonder what she is like, this here mate?"

Rhys walked madly over to a large window and looked out at the fiery surroundings that he adored.

Black crows hollered noisily outside. He put his hands together and a ball of light flew out and held straight into his palm. He muttered some words of forbidden to them dark magic, and then looked into the magnificent light. He could see his only brother and his weary new blood mate had just stepped through his part of the realm from theirs.

The power of the dark could only show him that area or else he would have used it to find... her.

His own one.

When the lass he had captured had said she was not into guys back then he had just assumed that she was playing hard to get with him at first speak, that was until she had flinched openly and had appeared frightened under his not-so-gentle first touch.

But now it was obvious she was telling the truth about who she truly was.

Because women all around fawned after him and his good looks and his –undiluted bristling power.

The one that no one would take from him. They could not have it.

"Let him try my dear. Let him try." He scoffed in disbelief. "Fess where are you; you fool!" He hollered in displeasure.

And with that, he left the room in a flustering hurry and slammed the door hard behind him as well, causing the walls to shake.

And the shadows followed adoringly behind him...

As Rhys stormed raging through the magnificent but also extremely creepy castle, spooky especially at night time, with the shadows that had awoken him, Fess popped out of nowhere like a bad smell.

"Ah, Fess." Rhys appeared rather pleased to see his kind of minion at the bottom of the stairway with an eager look to his whole being.

For once.

Not many stayed there in the castle with him and instead, they had their own magnificent homes nearby to go to, but the castle was big enough should they choose to stay there with him.

Most didn't. Rhys was not exactly the best of company during one of his crazy ass mood swings, even though those there in the darkness so admired and looked up to him as if he were their master and they were his puppets.

Which he kind of was.

"Sir." Fess respectfully bowed his head on seeing him storming his way frantically.

One of the only vamps that Fess confessed to admiring was the dark lord and their saviour- his saviour Rhys. Unlike that old jackass brother of his boss who had flung him out to go live in the darkness as if he were simply nothing and nobody! Simply dirt!

He hadn't deserved to be there!

He now obviously held a bad opinion of the younger Fortheart brother and wouldn't spit on him if he were on fire. One of the only ways to kill a vamp.

Not realising as he silently fumed that he would be seeing his old clan leader sooner than he would have liked…

Rhys licked his lips. A sneer went across his darkly, handsome face and his raging red eyes crossed straight over to Fess`s in less than an instant, "I saw something when I was dabbling in… shall we say the dark arts just before…"

"Sir?" The blonde-haired handsome Fess, but who appeared rather to be more brainier then he made out in Rhys`s eyes, in his view, appeared puzzled by what it could be that had been seen when he had brought the dark magic to the fold.

"My brother is on his way here to rescue the girl that I took from them before, with his new blood mate. It seems rather like he has turned his human mate into one of us. It is quite funny really; she looks tittering on the edge of madness as she craves the blood more than her own mate's sex. She will enjoy it here, for we have plenty and we are all mad."

"Oh." Fess grew quiet and wondered what that could mean for them all and he had just been thinking and fuming about his ex-leader and thinking bad thoughts of him.

It was only the second time that he had felt envy coursing through his very veins. The first time was when he was thrown out of his own home into the depths of the night, having to abandon his big, beautiful mansion that he so loved more than anything, and then shockingly threatened with annihilation if he did not leave that part of the realm.

For good.

To him that had been a vast overreaction. For hadn't they needed more vampire, soul collectors to join them?

To help them. And so, what if he wanted a bloody harem for his own? He was entitled to one!

Then the second time the envy grew due to learning that, that smuck Iden had found his fated mate.

And he hadn't.

The two that lingered in the stairway of the large, dark, and dingy castle both had something in common.

Their unyielding hate for Iden. Something that bonded them together.

Also, their shameless, endless but secret undying want and desire for a mate to complete them in every way that was possible. Even though she may possibly not be so.

"You seem quiet. What troubles you about it all, Fess?" Rhys rubbed his chin in deep marvellous thought. He could on occasion act concerned by his fellow vamps' plight and worry, but Fess never knew whether he was being genuine to him in question or else simply taking the mick as something to laugh at later when alone.

It could go either way and he wasn't very trusting from what he had seen of him so far.

Both were banished by that cretin Iden, rejected, still unmated and thrown into the darkness that wept with no tears. And Rhys had made Fess a fucking vampire in the first place! They had both made bad mistakes with women that they may a tad have regretted since then.

Just a tad.

Fess had back around about ten years ago turned stunning, voluptuous females to give him the power back that he thought he was owed. Owed from his unexpected death behind the wheel of a fast car.

A crash that was his own fault but that was by the by after having fell into a river on a night out first, dragging himself out. Now he was somewhere that didn't even have cars.

Nope, nowhere. They had wings after all, and the realm was not that vast so there was no need for them to own a motor vehicle or even a bloody bike!

He missed the buzz of driving along the country road. The roar as he drove to the ocean with the roof of his car down and the streets littered with people.

He had been rather popular when he was alive but with the fiery, dear sweet Elfina at his hip, he hadn't then looked another's way. And so, he had wanted that upon his death.

To be wanted.

Women flocking to his home for him to wine and dine and sixty-nine, after a day's frantic soul collecting. Friends knocking at his mansion door to hang out with, play games.

But it hadn't happened.

Not realising or even thinking how the woman that he had changed or tried to (the ones that survived the turning of course such as that moody cow, ungrateful Justina) would feel about being killed and then brought back to life as the undead.

Not thinking that those in the judgement realm on finding out had nearly put him down like a mangy dog with bowel ridden worms.

Rhys himself had taken Ruby on a whim. Half thinking that she was his destined mate when he had smelled that magnificent scent but half also knowing that she truly wasn't, because it all felt - flat.

Not what he had expected.

The sharp, hard slap that he had inflicted on her small, pearly shocked face had finally clinched it, although he was in too deep to back out of abducting her by then. And he wouldn't have given in to Iden by handing her back if it was the last thing that he did.

No. That would not do at all.

Because he knew that when he found his soul mate would not hurt a hair on her pretty head as he had done so that small but annoying Ruby when he slapped her into next week.

For there would be no doubt in his mind that she would be pretty, his one would so be.

Fearsome. A stunning, fiery woman that would make a fine vampire kind of queen to the darkness that Rhys so fucking loved more than anything else in the realms that it excited him without any words possible.

But that would change when she eventually came.

Wouldn't it?

He had at one time held love in his dark motionless heart. Had only ever loved, but four.

His parents, sister, and his stupid ass ungrateful younger brother. The rest of his family – dead, properly dead, and his brother was now lost to the grip of the goodness that encased most of the realm in its invisible hold.

Rhys would find his mate, he would claim her, chain her and she would not leave his side or talk to another male without him destroying the whole entire realm and everyone in it.

Everyone- except her.

He would do anything in his power to make that happen for his future bride to be his.

A crash brought him out of his gentle stewing and casual pondering.

Rhys did not think for a moment about what it was that had happened and instead only ran back to the large room that held Ruby in its dark clutches so that she could not leave there without pain.

Opening the door in a hurry, nearly taking the curved handle off he then stopped.

What was she bloody doing?!

Throwing a fireball that he created out of the palm of his hand near her head, she cried out in shock as it flew swiftly by, but no shame showing by her at what she was trying to do.

Trying to escape his clawed clutches. And no one but no one escaped. No one would make it out of there alive without his say so.

The small runty vamp appeared to have been trying to open the window to set herself free. And failing…

"What the fuck!" She cried and moved out of the way before she sadly became ash from the glowing fiery ball.

"What are you doing?" Rhys hissed angrily, his fists clenched tight, claws out into sharp talons, tempted beyond anything to prod her bare eyes out with them and eat them in front of her. Not that she would see it of course if he did!

That would stop her from trying to escape his clutches and the castle with no end. "There is no escape! Not for you, not for anyone but me!" He growled.

"I will try, even if it kills me on the way out." Ruby lowered her eyes nervously.

"Go ahead. Like I give a shit!" He scoffed. Because he didn't.

She muttered something un hearable until her breath. He felt like beating her with a broken broom.

And so, he went hurriedly over to grab her down from the window where she was now perched awkwardly on one of the huge sills. A massive scorch mark near her head.

Sadly, he had missed it.

But she could not escape though, even if she tried her fucking hardest and she must have known that when she managed to clamour up there– the dark magic around the castle, the shield that he had put up to keep her in and all else out temporarily would make sure of that one.

The very magic that kept him bordering on the state of madness, working for him and not against him.

As he gripped her, pulled her hastily down from where she had planned to escape from –

"Ow. Get off!" The dark-haired brat cried out. She kicked him where she thought it would hurt the most. His heaving balls and impressive long cock.

But didn't she know that nothing hurt him anymore? And it wasn't the black magic. It was all him. His emotions except his anger, had left him years ago never to return.

He had been that way a long time and there was no looking back.

"You!" A voice called out from behind. Stopping the two in their grappling tracks.

As Rhys pulled her to him, her remarkably tiny petite frame, he wondered how could he have thought someone as weak as her could be the other part of him? She most certainly wasn't!

Runty bitch!

She disgusted him in every way possible. Especially since that fine scent had vanished from her, and if it wasn't for Iden coming to rescue her then he would squash her like a dam bug!

But… he did not know what his future mate would look like or if she had been born yet. That thought alone made him shudder that she could still be a babe. And he would have to wait many more years. After all he was a monster not a peado.

But that he thought that this weak, defenceless, tiny female whose body resembled that of a developing teen, had been his mate!

No chance! No chance in the lower plain that she were!

Then as his eyes glinted remarkably hard, they both came crashing down in the large room, then they turned to the angry, no stunned voice.

It was Fess.

Ruby brushed herself down carefully, the stupid black frilly dress she had been placed in on arrival and glared directly at Rhys with a stern annoyed look. He returned the expression with no remorse. Then they both turned around and faced down Fess.

Something appeared to have shocked him there in the room and it wasn't Rhys and his nastiness.

He was evidently used to that by now.

"Fess!"

Ruby exclaimed as she then saw the owner of the shocked-sounding voice that awaited her at the back of her forced prison. "Is that you?" She asked quietly.

She squinted at the blonde vamp who had uttered the questioning words.

For the Fess she had known when alive were dark haired and curly-haired. This man was... his hair was blonde and straighter. But there was no doubt in her frazzled mind that it was still him, the same man. With dyed hair.

Hadn't he drowned? She remembered her sisters upset face at the news that her boyfriend had fell into a river and never to be seen again. His body had never been found, never surfaced to the world, so they had all assumed he had just drowned.

Divers had come up stumped also.

Well, this was clearly why!

He was dead. Or a half dead vamp any who.

Fess came running over to her on the floor in a graceful sprint. Not using his own magnificent wings to fly across the room in a crazy dash, but it had seemed that way with how quickly he had thrown himself across it madly.

His shoes clanked on the harsh ground as he landed at her feet.

"You... you're the girl that Rhys. Captured?" He asked cautiously looking at his leader now distastefully. His loyalties now shifting of wards. Obviously he had not been aware of who she were when their boss had gone and snatched her from the other side of the realm and brought her there.

Rhys simply rolled his eyes dramatically at all the drama soon coming his way like a targeting missile.

Did they have nothing better to do? It seemed not.

In answer she scowled straight at Rhys then nodded slowly at Fess in a silent answer.

"You... you know each other?" Rhys dared to ask the two as he looked from annoying brat to annoying minion.

She paused then turned to Fess, "There was a misunderstanding between us. He thought...and then now I'm here...and stuck it so seems by this... the bloody window wouldn't open either," She said snappily grimacing at her awful ordeal.

She then before she could utter anything else appeared to be going into a strange, hypnotic-like trance. Her eyes like glass. A parade of scanty blonde strippers could have danced through and all she would have done was stood there in her own spaced-out world.

"Is that a soul call?" Fess asked Rhys pointing, because it did not look like one with the way her eyes clouded over, looked glossy. Surely he thought that she shouldn't be having them as a prisoner? Or if she were then how would she do her soul collecting when she couldn't visit the human world to partake in her life's work?

She would be in big trouble.

Trapped by some kind of imposing magic and by Rhys in a dark eerie castle, like something out of the human's horror films. It was almost as if Count Dracula would pop out, out of nowhere and cause a fright to anyone that dared enter it.

"No."

Rhys squinted his eyes and walked over and prodded Ruby with a lone claw. He flicked her causing a small cut that healed over with her vampire healing. "That has been taken care of for a time, I promise you that lad." He simply said.

But still she did not look right even if that was, "Then why has she frozen still like that? Have you done something to her to make her that way?" Fess appeared to be uncomfortable that his previous acquaintance was in this frightful predicament. .

That caused Rhys to snap out, his eyes blaring bright, fangs out manically, "Careful Fess. I only treat you well because I like you somewhat, as we have much in common. If we fell out due to should we say thoughtless accusations, then…."

His mannerism grew accusing. This was a dance the two vamps had done many times before.

"Sorry. Sorry!" Fess pleaded with him his eyes wide in horror. Saying anything at that moment not to be tortured by him.

 Again. If it was not for his vampire healing then he would not have been able to walk for days after the last time that he had been struck, over and over as if their leader was not just punishing him for what he had done.

But what everyone else had also.

"No," Rhys said. "She has been doing that a few times since arrival. The darkness does not agree with her in the way that it agrees with me and you, because she has no badness in her. Sadly."

Fess exclaimed, "Oh, I see! The darkness doesn't agree with me either I must say, but I have no choice whatsoever in the matter what with your brother deciding to get me thrown out of the..."

"Blah, blah, blah. You are like a stuck record here Fess!" Rhys said angrily throwing his hands up into the air in abandonment. Fess shuffled nervously, obviously beginning to wonder if he had over stepped the mark with his sire.

"But it`s..."

"Silence! He is on his journey here. Iden is. So, you can take it up with him then if he can get through the shield. Until then..."

Then Rhys himself went into a trance that seemed to take a year for him to pass out of it. It could happen. The judgment realm signal could go on and on. And on. Other times the message was much shorter.

Fess simply sighed and waited standing awkwardly there, twiddling his thumbs anxiously. Glancing from Prisoner to the one who had put her there, one after the after until he began wishing that someone would snap out of their forced trance so that he could communicate things.

For he did not like being alone. It unsettled him.

One from the darkness, the other likely a message from the judgment realm. And he knew what Rhys would think about getting interrupted in the middle of a rant!

That would never do!

Rhys then suddenly snapped out of his trance with a fierce grimace. Muttering over and over again about 'fucking souls' that needed 'fucking seeing to', and then he looked as if he was getting ready to jump out of one of the large bay windows of the castle himself without another word uttered.

Ruby came too also with a shake of the head.

"Stay there." Rhys pointed.

She did not say anything, not a single word so he unleashed a fire ball that no matter how quick she tried to dodge it, she really just couldn't.

So, it hit her straight in the hand and she had no time to avoid it.

Nor could she have done. He would have seen to that!

But why? She hadn't deserved that. What a wicked vamp he were!

"Ow!" She cried in agony. Clutching her now charred hand in pain. Her hand now burnt through, the skin red and sore. Almost weeping as blister popped up and boiled.

"Stay there or that will be the rest of ya, you bloody muppet!" He gnashed his teeth in anger, and she stepped back in fear. Grabbing on to just air as there was nothing left to support her.

He then gracefully leapt out the window, his large black, bat-like wings opened as he fell swiftly down on his journey down to the human world to do his life's work, the one that must be done.

And to get away from there no doubt.

Fess knew without a doubt that Rhys hated his soul collecting with every fibre of his condemned soul, and that he always had done since the day he had last drawn breath. But he did it anyway.

Because they had to. There was no other alternative.

For it gave them a lifetime of being immortal after all and could they ever deny that?

"Has he gone?" Ruby murmured.

Still in pain, through tears that would not unleash to anyone.

Looking down at her now burnt beyond recognition, hand. As fire would never heal no matter how much she prayed it to, she cursed that good for nothing vamp as she eyed the scars that would stay there forever until her crumpled soul existed to be.

Still shaken too from the trance-like state that she had been unwillingly led to as the darkness edged closer to them all.

"I don't know what to do here Ruby."

Fess said this in all honesty through tired eyes that marred his handsome face. "Is there anything that will heal it?" Appearing unconvinced.

She shook her head in sadness, because there was not.

"It will never heal. That prick knew exactly what he was doing when he did it…"

Fess looked defeated at this speck of information. "I should have stopped him. I'm sorry." He said in all earnestly.

She knew straight away what he meant by this. As his girlfriend when alive sister, they had always had a good bond. Both were slightly mad, and adventurous, set in their ways.

In fact, if she was straight then they would have suited each other way better than he and Elfina had ever done.

Iden was truly the man that Elfina needed to boss over in the way that she liked to do. He would look after her until the end of time.

As a mate it was what was required of him.

Ruby gripped her hand aghast and shook her head. "It's ok, Fess. You did all you could there. I don't want to get you into any trouble. If you can't help me to leave then I will find a way myself somehow. Fetch me some water as I cannot even leave this bloody room!"

"But how? How will you do it?" He twitched and looked at the door and the window cautiously. As if frightened that Rhys would barge through either way, although with his soul collecting then he should be but a long while besides.

"I don't know."

She cursed that room that she was trapped in, that gloomy ass castle and the man that owned it all. She cursed his future mate whoever the poor sap actually were.

"He said Iden is coming here with his mate."

Ruby grinned.

"Omg. He found her!" She yelped excitedly up and down, trying to whoop but then remembering her whooping days were over now that her very lower arm and hand were charred to a crisp…

"Who? You know of her?"

"My sister. My sister is his fated mate. How cool is that?" But then it hit her, "Oh."

She said on sudden realisation that Fess was her sisters ex. And they had only been separated when he had inconveniently - died.

Awkward. She had really put her small foot in it hadn't she!

"Very cool." It clearly wasn't though, at all. But even through that he trundled on. "I`m helping you out of here still Ruby. For you and no one else besides that." No guessing who he was on about now, but it wasn't the time for hurt feelings all around.

Ruby grimaced as he brought the water over and she put her hand straight into it. "Fess. If you let me go then he will kill you. He will kill everyone in this bloody castle and then kill them again."

Fess looked at the door and gulped as the realisation hit.

"Per chance, I think you are right."

They would have to wait for her to be rescued until someone else came due to the forcefield. Due to the psycho vamp that would be back shortly and expected er there.

Because that was all they had.

CHAPTER TWO

<u>Justina</u>

She exited the judgment main building really, really slowly, after having not long carefully laid down the poor, departed soul that had been entrusted to her gently into the building that would make the final decision.

She had then patiently waited for them to be checked in and sent on their way to the elsewhere before she departed.

Well to the higher or the lower plains anyway. She sometimes did feel nervous for the lost soul that she met, and she often wondered discretely where they would then be placed and whether those in charge would make the right decision by them.

Asking herself would they place them where they truly deserved to be situated?

But she sadly would never know the outcome. The judgement realm was as far as they took them.

Where would her family go when they passed? That was if they were still alive. Her mum and aunt the only family she had for she had not been blessed with siblings much as she had wanted to of. She on the moment of her death and then her shocking resurrection, had decided not to taunt herself with the memories of her living family.

Iden had given her, the clan, them all one vital piece of advice – forget the family. At first she had been like how could she forget them? They were her everything! But no, he had been right all along. The urge of their blood calling her, the pain that they could not see her at all even if she wanted them to.

It was all too much. So, a few months after she had died she had silently said good bye to her kin forever and tried to make peace with her decision. In her mind it was the right thing to do and now there was no turning back once she had done it.

She would outlive them all, and the mourners at the funeral wouldn't even see her cry over it.

That was no easy thing to witness.

Justina paused for just a moment, her beautiful wings ruffling slightly in the late afternoon breeze as she looked tiredly around, trying to decide what to do next with herself.

Her blonde hair and glorious wings making her look oh surreal.

A part of her longed with every fibre of her being to return to her fabulous home in the vampire realm, hidden deep within the clouds, where she could then try to relax until the next mission that she was called to by a secret entity that no one knew of.

But she was loathe to work too late, knowing that lack of sleep would cause dark circles to appear under her immortal eyes and make her feel over a hundred years old and then some.

Which one day she would be. Still getting used to be immortal for it had only been ten years like this!

When she returned home then she could picture herself sinking into the cloud-like comfort of her bed, surrounded by plush pillows and silky sheets or her own crypt if she so chose. Most often she did not because she preferred the luxury of a bloody bed!

Becoming a vamp and no longer being human was still something that would take a while to get used to.

Or perhaps she wondered if she'd go out and meet her two best friends, laughing and chatting while sipping on chilled champagne and nibbling on hors d'oeuvres. Despite being a vampire, she revelled in good food and fun company in the same way that they both did.

Her friends were also without mates, just like her, and bitched also, so they relished in each other's company. But now that Iden had found his mate now, those carefree days of sex and revelry and sticking cucumbers up ones rear willing orifices, were gone forever.

She couldn't believe he had after hundreds of years stumbled upon his fated one out of nowhere - for their secret shagging arrangement had been perfect in her eyes. Hadn't it? She thought long and hard about it.

The sex, the secrecy, the getting one over on that annoying brat that he adored.

Yes, yes it had.

Although his fated mate would always take over preference for anything that the two of them could have had and one day it would just be a faded memory.

Now that it was sadly over, she did not know what the future would bring for her. Sure, she could eventually latch on to another up-and-coming leader, but what when he met his own fated one?

Then she would be stuck yet again.

The soul that she had collected, that she had feasted on hungrily before their last flight, the person`s first, was a middle-aged man who had tragically died of cancer. He had looked darn peaceful when he passed with an empty sigh, and she knew that he would go on to a better place after that and she had no doubt in her mind of it. No doubt at all.

Now she was thankfully full, satisfied, from his sweet but tangy delicious blood that hummed through her, that was in no way tainted by the tragic illness that he had sadly died with.

As she was preparing to go, for she could not stay there, nor did she even want to, then a strong blowing gust came from up above her as if a tornado was imminent.

Another soul would shortly be delivered.

She rubbed her arms as the chill grew over her and then decided to wait to see if it were anyone that she knew.

The vampire and not the soul.

A thud hit the deck. What the bloody hell was that!

She turned with a start as the hair on the back of her neck stood up in anticipation. Her blonde hair hung over her shoulder like she were some light bringing angel to the judgment realm. A realm at current only owned by eternal dwarves.

Dropping her wings back down behind her back so that for a moment she appeared to resemble a mere human. Not that humans could make it that far up without death.

Instead of a winged, invisible vampire from out of the stuff of fantasies. Or your worst nightmares...

She could see the back of them as they stood tall and proud. It was obviously a man.

A bloody huge one!

Wow. She wiped her drooling mouth. It was not the only thing drooling but it was a public place after all and while she might be invisible to humans, all these eternals around there could certainly see her!

He was muscular in his complete appearance, with a crop of long dark hair, black like a moonless night, that was tied back to presumably keep it from his chiselled face which she couldn't see clearly from her current position. Much as she wanted to.

He appeared to from the side that she could see to be sour, angry, as she watched his face turn into a grimace and he then crazily threw, yes threw, the poor soul of a lanky teenager a quarter of the size of he through the judgment court door as if it was made of paper!

Not even bothering to take it through carefully like she would herself do, and to make effort on its way to the vast unknown.

Wow, this vampire before her, this dish, this beast, was certainly beyond interesting. As if they had dared done that to a soul and gotten away with it! For only the lizard-like punishers that guarded the lower realms got away with bad behaviour since they were so beastly that no one, no one, dared to intervene in their bad mainly cruel ways.

So, for this guy, this gorgeous long, dark-haired prince, the blood-sucking, divine specimen to not be torn down at all for his lack of care for the souls.

He was then certainly something special indeed.

But then she gasped openly in sudden shock at the next notion. Clamming a hand over her mouth. As the huge, tall brawny man turned round as if to see the source of the shrieking noise that had escaped from her own surprised open mouth. She so then hid behind a large but extremely old pillar gripping onto it to steady herself as she trembled lightly.

She shook.

But not in fear – but something else entirely.

Desire. Every nerve lit up like Katie Perry's firework.

She had not felt this way since meeting Iden for the first time and personally, well personally she hadn't thought that what she felt for him, that she could feel that way again for anyone.

It hadn't been love but it was still something special while it had lasted.

She peeped around the pillar carefully with stunningly narrowed eyes as though not to be seen at all by anyone. For no one liked being spied upon did they? And with the rage that encircled this marvellous man then she strongly doubted that he did especially either!

He had thankfully for her stopped looking for the cause of the noise and was now turned to watching the soul be checked in from a distance as if he stayed so close to the dwarfs that he would catch some horrible, wilting disease that only he knew about.

Doing his job she supposed – yet half-ass.

She rather liked it!

As she watched him deep in wonder as a working dwarf strode over and spoke to him, she couldn't hear what they said. It seemed to strangely anger him somehow. So as the other male spoke to them a ginger spiked dude that she did not know of then, he kicked the wall of the humungous white glorious building, leaving a huge crack in it from his obvious power.

From the foot of it to the bottom.

She felt the power radiating off him when he kicked out as if he were a beacon of strength and instinctively she now knew that he was far older than her own ten years as a vampire.

But how old was he? In the vampire world age gaps didn't matter so much because some could be thousands of years old and look only twenty-five. She would have been forty now if she was a human, but still looked the thirty that she had unfortunately been the age that she had died at.

She watched him intently, admiring the grace with which he moved with a masculine arrogant swagger and there was no way that she could not miss how his eyes seemed to penetrate the darkness of the night into his every being. Around this man, certainly no gentleman, hung an unfamiliar scent, one she never had encountered before: . She sniffed and her eyes shone a shade of red.

Mmm... he smelled musky like fresh leather and sweet like honey. It clung to every part of her being and drew her into this unknown man. She could spend all day basking in that unworldly fragrance!

Despite her fear of his immense power that he held, that was he, she couldn't help but feel a thrill at the prospect of being so close to something so ancient and powerful.

So sexy.

Her heart if it beat would have fluttered madly in her ample chest. Desire lit her soul up like a light bulb from her head, down her spine until it reached her most secret place and back up again.

Not wanting to let up.

For something was drawing her to the other vamp just like they were entwined together as one for all of eternity. She knew now that she would not go home, go down to the earth but she would follow him, yes, that's what she would do.

See where he went, who he talked to, what clan was his one. Did he have one? Some vampires were wanderers and that was without the few earth dwellers. She doubted he was an earth dweller!

The humans would certainly be in trouble. She then felt a pang at hoping that he wasn't an earth dweller. After all it had taken ten years for her to bump into this… fine thing.

The one that made her feel all woman and she did not yet know why. Maybe she was a hussy after all? Because the things she wanted this beast to do to her were in no way at all lady like! They were as far from a lady as one could truly get.

Maybe he was mated?

Some poor fucker chained to a bed no doubt! She wouldn't mind being at the end of that one! But no, no he wasn't her mate she argued with her inner being as his smell overwhelmed her.

As she stared at him, her eyes straight roamed up and down over his pure divine muscular form, taking in every amazing, sculpted detail, from the bulging veins on his arms to the sharp angles of his curved jawline.

With a sudden urge to get closer so that she could breathe him in, breathe it in, she inhaled deeply and caught a whiff of something intoxicating again.

Her heart raced as she realized what it was - this angry, storming-around man was most certainly - her fated mate.

No, it could not be! Why now? Why here? Why him?

But it were likely true. Destiny was knocking on the door, and it was calling her name for her to answer it. NOW.

As she tensed up then a feeling of peace washed over her, tug of longing pulled her towards him where she felt like she might possibly belong, and she stepped forward without conscious thought that she was stepping towards a monster.

Her and her alone.

Suddenly without noticing her, he leapt into the air like Superman on serious steroids, his powerful wings unfurling to keep him aloft in the misty air.

She watched him for a moment as he soared even higher, she marvelled at his incredible strength and agility hidden so very deep - he was like nothing she had ever seen before or likely ever would in all her days as a blood sucking vamp.

She must see where he went.

She must! Because if she did not then she might never see him again and that would not do! Then she would spend an eternity doing something that she hardly ever did – weeping with sorrow.

Pain would run through her at never seeing such a marvel again.

Justina trailed along behind him but slightly slower as they both soured like giant birds through the now dimming sky.

Close enough so that she could follow him a short while behind, but not near enough that if he stopped even for a brief moment in his path, looked round, that she would be caught in his gaze by him, and landing in anger`s way.

Her own wings she could see were more angel-like than his ferociously flapping bat ones. What would she give for them to wrap around her and keep her held in place so that they were moulded together in all of infinity?

Trapped in his huge, muscled arms forever.

But wait. She shook herself from her fantasies.

The sky was changing as they neared the hidden vampire realm. The sky slightly blurred as the realms entangled into one another, and then they were now what she now called home.

The vampire realm.

Her home for the past decade. And forever more.

It was a magical place. A whole new world almost like.

How strange it had been when she had taken her first flight through the Earth`s sky. She had been human and then suddenly she could bloody well fly through the sky!

Now it was like second nature.

She looked over at the gorgeous beyond anything male who had now safely landed onto the ashy looking floor. Still lost in his own world to see hers was closer than he so thought.

Could it be, could it really be him? Would he like what he saw when he eventually realised that the ballsy, blonde female was his oh-so-destined one?

One that was trailing along behind in absolute awe at her future vampire daddy.

She feared so.

She felt like a nothing and nobody to him even at the distance they shared or would do when they finally met.

She looked around and then mad panic overwhelmed her so much that the male, her one, was temporarily gone from her spiralling thoughts and desires.

This was the actual darkness!

Not the time of day, but the darkness that 99% of vamps feared of. She was here!

If she stayed here in this place, then the darkness she would become.

The dark and evil part of the vampire realm that no one with half a brain cell would willingly walk into!

Or fly by to have a quick nosy. Home of the banished and the dark, dodgy, and depraved. Which she most definitely wasn't! Yet...

She might be when their leader found out where she had just been! Iden would blow his fuse at the whole idea of one of his clan venturing where he had told them not to go.

But she herself for the first time just had flown into it as if it was her second home and not a holiday one.

Crap.

So, then who was that guy she wondered?

She gulped as she realised that she was then right, that it was likely that the guy who had caught her eye, caught her ever-lasting desire, her wants, her needs, and who was 99.9 per cent her eagerly awaited fated mate of all time was not just likely some bad boy vamp who had come crashing along into her heart.

He was more than likely evil as well from where he had just roughly landed as though he owned it…

Like a comedic villain on the children's ward tv.

But then something unexpected, "Why are you following me my pretty?" She heard him say in question to her in an extreme state of agitation.

She gasped and he simply laughed wickedly.

Shit. He must have seen her sneaking around behind him!

She needed to get out of there. Fast. Plus, she now grew thirsty. And she knew that this guy would not let her leave in any kind of a hurry so that she could quench her creeping in anxious thirst!

She turned to abruptly leave that dreadful place, to leave him though she did not want to at all, she mused that she must. Her body at war with itself.

But she would be back. Darn it she would!

Of course, she would. Her want for him, the fact they were both truly destined would just have to wait.

Just as she went flying off into the sunset, she was grabbed hard from behind and so landed hard backwards in someone`s huge, rippling but firm arms.

His.

Oof!

She made to leave, to turn away, her blonde hair flickering behind her under the near moon light, but there was no way that he would not let up and he instead dug his claws in even tighter.

She could now see as she gazed that they were quite near to a magnificent but gloomy ginormous castle, but it seemed to have some kind of forcefield around it protecting it.

A yellow tinge showed where it began.

She had heard about this horrible place from more than one person in her lifetime and knew without a doubt to keep away from there at all costs.

Iden's scummy, demented bad brother lived there with Fess her creator.

If she saw him again, then she would slap him into next week for what he had turned her into!

A fucking monster!

But first… she had been caught and it was not looking good for her. This was someone far worse than Fess…

Fuck.

A breath sniffed her neck from behind as though it was sniffing its upcoming dinner. She shivered all over as the fear left her and she suddenly felt a wonderous craze at the sniffers owner.

Desire shamefully coursed through her at the thought of being eaten up by this god-awful vamp man, devoured.

And spat out again for him to have more. He did not appear the sort to waste a drop of his meal. As she oozed for him.

She knew someone like that would not be like Iden who liked to be dominated in the bedroom by his women. A submissive male.

Now one.

He instead, this male here would be the dominator. He would absolutely take her, thrust hard into her with his thick unforgiving cock, with no mercy at all behind it as he likely held her arms tightly behind her back, so that she could not move as he pounded into her with every thrust.

He would simply just… own her.

For always.

And she no doubt would let him and take great pleasure in it.

"Where the fuck do you think you are going?"

This vamp was angry. Really angry now. It was as if steam was coming out of his elfin like ears as she made to escape her doom.

And her fate…

"I…I…" Her mouth did not want to answer this intimidating specimen that gripped her in more ways than one. She froze.

"What trickery is this?" The rugged man then groaned as he threw her to him with a blast of something extra.

Magic.

Now she was gripped in his dark gaze from which she could not break free from. His hooded eyelids that held magnificent stormy eyes that blazed.

"Who are you to come here into my domain with all your precious beauty, and then to leave me? How dare you even try to escape my clutches!"

Heck, even his deep, mysterious, snarly voice was drool worthy! So full of imploding rage but also at the tip of it was so full of want. Desire, lust. Craving...

For her.

She wanted it in return so very much.

She did not know whether he had smelled her fate ness on her skin. Or if he chose to ignore it.

"There is no trickery here. But I need to leave here sir. Please I must." She flinched then elbowed him hard in the side because nothing else would surely do with this angry beast, pushing past him and made to go but he took her again into his arms and laughed wildly at her expense.

He pierced through her.

"Can it be true this time? And such a beauty at that who comes to my door? One that belongs to me and not to another? One that will warm my cock, as well as my dead beatless heart into finally beating a tune..."

Wow.

He put a finger through her glittery blonde hair in caress and stroked her crimson cheek with a sharp claw that dug in slightly with a graze.

What could those claws do she wondered as her own, purple-tinged blood dripped down her cheek in which he licked off her soul?

"Your... your door?" She stuttered out, shocked that the castle was his.

Gazing around at all the lava flowing right near the gigantic castle, the dark fearsome, fire breathing dragons, and the stark raving mad unicorns with horns that could brain someone if they trod to close.

Were those magnificent creatures always that way she wondered as she watched them shriek and try to frantically mate with each other?

Having never seen them before.

Beautiful.

Or were they consumed into madness just like it appeared her fated mate had been since lingering there in the darkness? His apparent home. Maybe he too had always been that way. Probably why Iden kept his clan firmly away from there. A hero, but she did not want a hero. No, she wanted – this. Whatever it were.

She owned her own horse and kept it near her home. Her Cedrik. She knew that the rest of the clan would keep an eye on him when she herself could not do. Horses were quite common there in their realm and not for food but for merely companionship.

Jack Russell's were certainly not common.

A volcano bubbled wildly in the background that looked like it could go at any minute. A real-life bloody volcano that could burn them all into ashes! Eat their flesh as though they were never there.

Did this fearful guy throw his enemies into there?

Probably.

Maybe he would throw her in? She gulped. Not thinking so.

She was now no longer the bossy, confident, bitchy strong woman that flaunted herself proudly around the vampire realm, confidence fluttering behind her.

"Hmm. Well, I suppose it is our door now, my sweet one." He sniffed her again shamelessly and groaned out in a state of extreme pleasure as her scent drove him wild.

Wilder.

"I can't believe it, I can't!" He growled.

Swinging her sharply around to face him.

Their eyes locked together. Her soul nearly did too. "And my god you smell so sweet! Like honey. My honey." He hissed with possession.

He would possess her!

So, it was true then that they were fated she thought as a pit of realisation hit her stomach. Because that was the exact scent that he had smelled of and he now had said the same.

His eyes appeared to be from what she could see were nearly always permanently red. Not like the usual vamp whose eyes only changed when full of raging anger or after downing the sweet human nectar.

A light bulb tinged in her frazzled brain.

"Oh, my god. You're Rhys, aren't you?" It finally dawned on the blonde vamp who her fated one were.

He naughtily sniggered in response and leaned in even closer. "Oh, you know of me? Am I famous in your parts my fair one? I wouldn't believe everything that you hear though darlin." He mooched forward and kissed her on the cheek with possession, so that she was marked by him and him alone.

He pined to kiss her all over until she smelt only of him and his essence.

She would smell only of him!

As a vampire, the marks would eventually fade from sight though.

She did not pull away. She would stay.

It was decided.

She felt like she were in ecstasy as his lips brushed her soft, velvet skin. He nipped the flesh with his teeth. His tongue teased her as it swirled round.

She put a hand on her hips.

"Everyone knows of you, Rhys. I just didn't put the two together to realise who you were. I just thought you was a nobody, an outcast." She sniggered, but inside she knew she was pushing it with this fiend.

And him.

What would it take for this man to crack? To watch him become irate and unleash his power to everyone until they all ran away screaming and crying?

He studied her, "Well, you know now. As it will be the only man's name that you ever utter in your lifetime again. Or else." His eyes blazed a deeper red as though the idea of her doing so made him want to go on a rampant killing spree.

Bathe in their blood.

Was he for real? What a chump! She internally rolled her eyes to the sky. Then glanced at him again.

Oh, he was serious. Deadly serious.

She rolled her eyes for real now. Causing him to grip her jaw. Hard.

"Careful mate. It is only because of who you are that I will let you off from treating me that way." He pushed his lips to hers and tried to slide his tongue into hers. Wanting hers to meet him.

She pushed away; she would not give in to this deranged monster. The one that would give all vampires a bad name. Even though she did not want to.

"Hmm. Playing hard to get? Now that will not do. Not do at all!" He pulled her arm tightly back until she winced openly. Not enough to break it, but enough to make her stop in her tracks.

Halt.

"No." she tutted. "Get off my arm you bloody Einstein!"

He shuddered, "Give me your name. So that I will know what to call out with abandonment each and every night when I spill my release when we are apart. Although if I have my way, that shall never be the case."

"No."

"Tell me."

"Justina." She said cautiously. Should she have?

For giving a man like that her name was giving him power over her. Far more than he already currently had. And she was already finding it hard not to stare at him in complete and utter awe as his essence consumed her.

"Beautiful." He said huskily. "I thought that my mate would be the one to finally see me. But luckily for me – you already do."

"No thanks to your pal, Fess."

He frowned deeply.

But then before she could respond further or him show his disgust for there would be no hurt from the likes of him, that she had pushed him away.

A voice spoke out from the darkness.

They both whipped their necks around so fast, and he let go of her briefly.

But not quite. He still had a hold, as he now forever would do. Until one of them died or they likely killed the other one in a jealous rage or when he pounded her to death when they entwined.

It was Iden hidden away in the shadows who spoke.

With a panting Elfina. You could see, anyone could see, that she was fading fast and furious and needed the energy of human blood sooner rather than later as he practically held her up with his gentle hold.

He would not let go. He would see to it.

CHAPTER THREE

"I have not come to fight you brother. We just want Ruby home where she belongs and then we will be on our way." The younger one said hesitantly. Fearing the darkness and on edge for his brother and his rage.

Justina supposed that she should feel jealous of the way he gripped his mate oh so very tight and possessively to his skin. As though she were a comfort coat and he wanted to wear her.

For it was not that long ago that she had bedded this handsome man who now belonged only to another as he forever now would. But she found the feeling that she expected to come.

It didn't.

Not even a hint of it. She felt purely – nothing.

When they were at the put-together last-minute clan meeting, she had felt extreme anger at what their leader had to say to them all that fateful night. A mixture of pent-up rage, scorn, and most of all – total embarrassment from being kinda dumped.

Not even doolaly Dorothy killing her husband had taken away the hurt that she had felt lingering.

Now there was simply… nothing.

Zilch.

And she knew that it wasn't because of the weak, limp, female vampire but simply beautiful, brunette, new baby vamp that was now being propped up by her destined fella. The one who gazed at her with an overly worried expression as she appeared to spiral deeper and deeper into blood deprivation that could be her undoing.

Justina had seen that before and it wasn't pretty.

No. It was - because of Rhys and who he now was to her.

Her Rhys. Her mate.

Gosh, it felt weird for her to even think that thought in her mind, let alone say that out loud! To have someone that she would be tied to for the rest of her days.

Forever.

Someone like him. Someone – evil.

But she could feel the blazing heat of him next to her as he pressed into her possessively so that she could feel every muscle, even the more tighter when his brother spoke out to them.

Interrupting the new mates from getting to know one another.

His bulge she reckoned needed its own postcode as she could feel it press firmly into her as though it wanted to seek her out, and to make her insides its new home.

To take her and to never let up even if she begged, cried, and screamed for him to. She would love that. She knew that he would do but there was a long way to go until she would trust this wicked vamp behind her.

She wondered what it would look like in the flesh if she ripped his trousers down and stuck it right in without delay.

Feel like. Taste like. Salty maybe?

She knew that it would taste divine.

Also, slight shame hit her due to her having gone from one brother and on to the next.

She wasn't a complete and utter hussy after all! For how the hell was she to ever know that fate had played a humorous game by putting her with one brother and then her really being fated to the other?

Ones that hated each other.

She wasn't psychic after all…

Rhys finally let go of his fated one although you could tell it pained him to.

"Stay there." He ordered her with no qualms. His eyes burned like a fire that only she could extinguish with her very being, her very essence. She gasped at them in complete amazement, locked in with his crippling stare that threatened to be the undoing of her.

"But I…" She said defiantly.

"You will do as you are told or else face the consequences my fair one…" He smirked smugly. Knowing that she would obey him in every way that there were. Wouldn't she?

She would.

This whole look it caused her to shudder openly. What would one of his punishments be like she wondered as she stared down at his hefty bulge? Would she enjoy it as he bent her over and spanked her until her bottom went red with his handprint etched on her dainty skin?

For sure she would. Who wouldn't?

"Justina? What are you doing here?" Iden asked as he suddenly spied her ducking her head out of the way so that she couldn't be seen by the others that approached them with an important task on their minds. Having taken a long while to even notice that she was even in his vicinity, she had finally been spotted.

Not used to being unsure for she had a face that sadly everyone remembered.

Elfina gripping carefully to his arm with a long glance the blonde beauty's way. Justina unfortunately had that way with women she had sadly found in all her days. She knew the beauty that she so possessed, a beauty which had been the only reason that Fess had turned her into a vampire in the first place!

For a crazy ass harem.

And she was aware that female vamps often gave her a wide berth because of this beauty that she could not help owning. It had been like that in the human world, here was no different.

"Do not even look at her. She is mine! And mine alone!" A hiss cried out to them all. Stating his ownership to the blonde.

Before she could say anything more, her other part said this possessively. Going straight in for them all to know who this model-like creature belonged to.

He now owned her. She was his. No one would take her away. If they did – they would surely die.

"Who is this?" Elfina asked in confusion as the two brothers glowered either side of her.

Weakly perhaps. Her eyes were now a shade of washed-out tired pink. Like when you have a hangover and haven't slept a wink all night, even when you knew that you probably should.

That look.

"I am one of your mate's clan. One of your clan I guess now," Justina simply shrugged awkwardly and turned away from her clan leaders new chosen one.

Because she was.

Still was part of the clan, part of where she belonged. Would always be.

The darkness was not meant for her, and it would never be who she was or what she was about. Rhys must understand that. No way could any normal vamp take pride in this god forsaken place. She herself would rather die than spend eternity there.

Oh wait…

"Not anymore!" This was Rhys. "You are in my clan now." His muscles rippled as he strained for dominance over her and everyone standing there in his part of the vampire realm.

He was the biggest one there. Even if he wasn't it did not matter- he was in charge there.

He was the darkness's master.

"Yes, I am." She argued. Who the heck did he think he was?! She fumed inside.

"No. You will find you are not. Not anymore. Your place is now with me, at my side. As my one." Rhys had hold of her again in a tight grip, but it did not hurt as though he was trying to be gentle somewhat.

The way that he gripped her he was unlikely to let her go.

To keep her prisoner where he thought she belonged.

He smelled her softly, nuzzling her. His lips nipping at the bare part of her skin on her neck.

"Are you ok Justina?" Iden asked in her defence. Probably wondering why his elder brother was trying to gobble her up like a turkey at Xmas!

Vampires loved Christmas.

She had forgotten for a moment that he were even there in their midst. Her mind elsewhere but there.

"Don't ask." She said quietly in a whisper to her leader, old leader, who knew? Then shrugged.

"Don't even speak to her!"

Oh dear.

Rhys had a look on him where he looked like he would kill his own granny if she dared even speak one word to her, even for not but a single moment.

"Can someone tell me what is going on?" Elfina asked, in a whisper. Clearly full of exhaustion and puzzled like anything.

Iden shrugged unknowingly and then looked briefly at his brother and Justina for clues to what the bloody hell was happening. His gaze only gazing for a moment over Justina's as though not to anger the two others.

Then after a pause Iden replied, "No, no way in hell. She is yours? You are his? Dear god almighty!" The penny had well and truly dropped for them all. Well, him anyway.

"Oh. So... I'm figuring it out now. This crazy man is mated to this blonde lady that looks like a super model," Elfina said as she also started to also understand the situation that was panning out before her.

Now appearing sorry for the blonde instead of jealous.

"I don't care a fuck what the fates say about us. I am doing this existence alone." Justina said defensively. To them all but mainly to herself.

"I don't blame you." Sighed Iden at the thought of his former fwb being mated to his own brother. "But Justina, this changes everything. You know it does. You are where you need to be. With whom you need to be with."

She shook her head in refusal.

"It doesn't. Look you owe me nothing now that... you know..." She nodded towards Elfina who frowned at the gesture. Trying to read into it if she could.

"What exactly are you two?" Elfina grew suspicious at the two's defenceless body language around her. Wondering if they had been something more not something less. For Elfina even though she had a curvaceous figure she did not have the super model looks that Justina possessed and the confident nature to go with it.

Her nose wrinkled in sudden displeasure at the thought of her own mate with this stunning blonde creature before her and her expression became frosty.

Her eyes darkened.

No one, but no one wanted to anger a baby vamp. It could be their undoing. A baby vampire`s wraith would make the darkness look like a kids playground.

"That is the past my love." Iden insisted as he noted her face darkening into something that was not quite her. Still getting to know his one and only soul but knowing that that look was frightening him into settling her.

He tried to defuse the situation, "No offence." Aiming this remark at Justina who rolled her eyes unashamed.

"No offence taken!" She said snarkily then tried to distance herself from them all.

She wanted out. Now.

She needed time, needed space. It was all becoming too much!

Wishing that she hadn't followed this impressive beast to this awful destination and had instead chosen to go back for an early night of peace.

And after this revelation, after the truth about Iden and Justina was out, was when Rhys became a true monster out of everyone's darkest nightmares.

There was no hint of the man inside him for he now just became enraged with undeniable anger. The madness at learning that his fated had been with his own brother sexually, made him leap in the air and leap for his kin with a strong desire to kill him.

Not needing any weapon. For he himself was the weapon!

He would destroy anyone that kept him from her. Almost frothing like a rapid dog on heat.

As Iden was yanked firmly away from her, Elfina who had been using him a kind of crutch then staggered back and fell onto the ground in a heap. Crying out as she stumbled from lack of blood. Knowing that really she should have stayed back at her new home.

At seeing his mate fall, Iden pushed his warring brother away from him to get right to her, his beatless heart wild in panic. But the other one was too full of impending enraged anger to stop trying to kill his own flesh and blood anytime soon.

Iden`s previous lust could be his undoing.

"Rhys just stop! Now!" Justina snapped.

She tried to step near her leader, but her mate snarled in warning for her to back off. Even at his own fated one. Not wanting her caught between him and his brother, in jealous sibling rivalry.

He wanted to keep her safe. He needed it. Nothing could happen to her. To wait hundreds of years and to have it there in his grasp, he would be a mad man to lose it forever now.

Rhys looked at her his eyes flickered from anger to something softer, he became like a man again, but then before you know it they turned red as if he himself was the danger to them all standing there.

Although now poor precious Elfina was no longer standing of course. Still collapsed on the floor, the rest unable to help her.

"You and him!" The long-haired warrior screamed at his younger brother who had the sense to look ashamed of what he had unknowingly done when he had plunged his cock in another.

Looking so almighty and powerful, fierce, that now Justina only felt proud of her future man, if she chose him to be that way. And slightly scared of what he could do to the others once he got his claws into them.

At war with herself about where her loyalties lied.

For Elfina yes, she did not know her, but she was innocent in all of this. She not long ago was only human.

Justina knew that this crazy, fuming vamp would not hurt her, not intentionally for he must feel the pull of the bond that she did, that tugged her to them. The one that sang right through her. Only to her.

And only to him.

The bond that made every fibre in her being, crave this dark, delicious, and extremely deranged man. The one that would fight for her, as he was fighting for her now.

Who likely always would. And she would let him. But she could not be with him. She would run, and he would chase her. And she herself would let him.

"I have a mate now. So do you, so does she. So, this is over just nothing brother!" Iden tried to explain to his older brother but not knowing quite how to find the words.

"So Elfina..." Rhys started.

"Don't." Iden warned. Knowing what his brother would say. Telling him that he would tell his mate his greatest secret in return for his own brutal banishment.

One that was truly deserved.

"Fuck off!" Rhys sneered. "Elfina… did you know that old Iden here…"

"Rhys! Don't you dare…"

Oh, he dared alright!

"Old Iden here killed himself. I brought him back from half way down a cliff and he still punished me by sending me here to rot. Anyone would think that he wasn't thankful! My weak ass brother. Coward." He spat.

Everyone's heads whipped around at vampire speed in one direction, and one direction only. The elephant in the room now appearing in all its grey glory.

Elfina looked at him, her skin clammy and pale and then suddenly having got up spoke "Is this true?", then she fainted.

Iden tried so desperately to get to her before she fell onto the ground, to help in only the way that he could do so, but Rhys was trying to firebomb him right then with more than malicious intent, and so he was far too busy dodging himself out of the way.

For if he died then who would help Elfina?

Would Justina?

One false movement and he would be toast! For Rhys had more power than most.

But then before Justina could react as the baby vamp fell, who was debating about helping them or not, someone quickly swooped down and picked up Elfina in their beefy arms and ran, no flew, off with her at the speed of light.

That quick that they only saw the glint of his straight blonde hair in the approaching moon light as they took the clan leaders fainted mate away.

From him.

"Fess!" Cried Iden enraged on working out who it were. His monster then instantly reached the surface in an instant at its mate being taken from them, his cries likely heard for miles upon miles as it screamed in empty pain.

It`s empty arms.

The humans wouldn't know what had hit them once the sound travelled to their land!

He tried to leap after them, to save his fated one who was dying it seemed, but his warring brother was not done with him quite yet and grabbed his leg, holding on with sharp claws.

And so, he would not let up.

Rhys threw him right back down where he felt that he belonged and stood on his brother's head with a large, studded boot so that Iden wiggled underneath him, gearing to be let go to retaliate.

Once he was done.

Or maybe he never would be done with him.

He appeared undecided by it.

Justina tried to give Iden a hand in which Rhys ripped it firmly off. Angered as though it had been a cock and not merely a hand touching her, "No touching!" He grimaced, "Mine. All mine!"

She chose to ignore him and to keep trying to help her clan leader back up. Her mate might own them all, but certainly not her.

Iden - Weakened by the only one that could weaken him – his blood brother.

His cursed one.

She tried to stop the fighting between Rhys and Iden. This wasn't how she wanted to spend the rest of her evening, in the middle of two scrapping immortal men.

Her sort of ex and her new found mate.

"Look Iden, Fess is a prick I will give him that, but she should be safe with him. I guarantee it!" She smiled warmly at her new mate to make up for talking to his brother which she knew he did not like one iota.

Hoping that he would believe her pleading words because she herself was not quite so sure that Elfina would be all right.

Fess didn't have her heart anymore. In fact, no one did.

Rhys found the opportunity to taunt his brother in to more of a frantic frenzy, "Yes, your mate is safe with her ex. How lovely." Rhys smirked in triumph joy as he grinned evilly. His handsome face now marred by his spite, as his human like form came back to life and his inner monster left.

He would not let anyone run off with his mate and let them live to tell the tale of it like Iden had!

They would cry for decapitation once he was done with them. Heck he would fuck Justina hard on their grave!

The dark master was the strongest out of all the vampires after all.

He could do what he wanted, as he pleased. Anyone that didn't know this was stupid or had a death wish.

Iden now got off the floor in an instant. The thought of his mate with another man gave him the surge of power that he so very needed right then.

He flipped the other one over in a brutal instant.

"Get off of me Rhys. Imagine if this was you and you were me and your mate had been taken! Have some empathy even though every emotion that you used to possess seems to be now long gone."

Rhys glowered. "I imagine that heads would be rolling, and they would not have the hands to touch anything ever again." Turning to Justina, "Now my queen, go and wait in the castle for me and I will finish things off here with my brother. In all finalty." Emphasizing the finished. Deliberately or accidentally, one was not quite sure.

"Finish off like to patch things up, or to finish off as in actually finishing him off?"

A good question.

"You care for him?" An angry brow shot up in question. Not wanting to know or hear the answer. He stuck his clawed hands into his palms and watched the purple blood drip down onto the floor.

"No, no." Yes, yes. She didn't know! "Take the force field down for me 'mate' and I will meet you inside. No arguments. I promise you." She gave him a small smile that did not reach her eyes.

Her fated one uncharacteristically nodded eagerly.

"You will come with me willingly then?" Her fated asked with a small smirk.

"Look I don't know about that! We hardly know each other Rhys. I like sex as much as the next person but slow down a minute big boy!"

She jested, rambling on nervously as his eyes pierced into her now non-existent soul. The one that had been destroyed by Fess and Fess alone.

She hoped that Elfina gave him what for when she broke free! But after seeing the new vampires struggle with her newness she knew that it would be highly unlikely that she had much to put up any sort of fight with her keen and willing abductor.

"Hmm well, we fuck when I say we fuck? Got it?"

"Tiny bit rapey there aren't we big boy." She shrugged no plussed and made to leave the realm.

As she moved away he watched her as she reached the castle, she felt him. She didn't need to look around for he was just there.

"Give me ten minutes brother." He winked at Iden who was frozen on the spot. Unable to move. She presumed with dark magic again.

Iden did not say a word. For how could he?

CHAPTER FOUR

Rhys gripped Justinas arm with all his might. He dug his claws in until her purple blood dropped. He pulled it to him and licked the blood clean up. Leaning forward so that they were cheek to cheek, again...

"Now listen here 'mate' I am a monster but also a monster I am not. I would not have to as you put it - rape you. I only want the screams that come from your mouth to be ones of the upmost pleasure and not ones from any pain otherwise. Do you understand me?"

He nibbled her cheek and then made little bites up her throat. She shivered in secret enjoyment.

"Yes...." She did now.

"Now then, I find going round the back way would be best. For what I have planned for you now before you go into the castle on your merry way then I doubt you would not want my brother and all the darkness to see. Or perhaps with your history. Maybe you would?" A tilt of his chiselled jaw.

Justina sighed.

He was not going to let that one go anytime soon! She simply followed him without a word. Trying not to get turned on as he licked her blood from his swollen naughty lips. Knowing that unlike human blood he did not need it to survive, but that his obvious adoration for her made him lean towards that way.

Towards the back was a massive door, obviously the back entrance to the dubious castle. She eyed the ginormous volcano that bubbled not subtly at all nearby as though it wanted to take them out at any given minute should it choose to.

She nodded towards it, "How do you live near that thing? How do you live... here in the darkness?"

He said simply. "It is my home, as you yourself now are." He then pointed at her flowing dress that lifted slight as a breeze tore through. "Take your knickers off."

"What?" She froze on the spot. But not surely frozen and made to stay there but frozen with his wild words.

Rhys scoffed, "Oh, are you hard of hearing? I said take those knickers off. Now."

This vamp would be the death of her...

She was beginning to wish she had flown off at the first chance that she had. Instead of meekly obeying her new mate and pottering off to the dark, gloomy castle like it was some kind of adventure. This thing coming, her adventure could either be her being impaled but in a good way, or else a bad one.

"What! No… You can't make me…" Justina pleaded.

"You will but only because it is what we both want."

"Big head."

"Indeed…" A sure grin.

She looking all around in every direction slowly pulled her knickers down and giving him eye contact all the while, and she kicked her legs out of them. Gulping nervously at his breath now at her back in rapid pants as though he were desperate for her to get them off.

She wasn't taking them off slowly as if she was doing a strip tease for him, but instead out of sheer nervousness at why he wanted her to even take them off!

After all she reckoned that he wanted to punish her in every way so possible. But she would fight back! He would not win.

Unless she let him!

He grabbed the silky knickers straight from her and sniffed them hard. Then as her eyes bulged and her cheeks if they could, would have blushed hard in embarrassment. He naughtily as she watched in horror began nibbling on the gusset to presumably see if he could lick up every loose drop that had left herself.

Then she watched as before her, he got onto his knees, prized her legs swiftly apart and then as she gulped went on to stick his face right into her core as though she herself was what he needed to breathe.

Justina gasped in pleasure and looked down at the awe-inspiring vamp. She swore she could see a grin down there as his head met the spot and his red darkened eyes met hers.

"Wha…what are you doing?" She groaned between his fearsome licks of her cunt. Shuddering at each nibble. Being eaten alive at the back entrance to the castle, no pun intended, and actually enjoying herself.

 A lot. Legs shaking, nearly quaking she just hoped that no one rounded that corner…

He pulled away. "What does it look like I'm doing? Having a spot of lunch with my mate." He groaned happily as though he was enjoying it as much as she were, then stuck his head straight back under her dress and carried on feasting on her dripping wet cunt.

He licked, nibbled, teased, and taunted while she wantingly wiggled in shocked delight. Sometimes reaching the spot right away and at other times missing it as though to make her groan in sheer anticipation that he would get to it. After a while of this she moved his head to keep it exactly where she wanted it!

At her bulls eye!

He feasted and as she started screaming in pleasure - he stopped, got up and shoved her knickers into her mouth as a sort of gag.

Then lowering himself he finished his job off. Oh well - nearly. "Who am I to you? My Justina..." Rolling his tongue at the end of his words.

"Please, don't stop. Don't tease me like this!" Her legs shaking as she felt like she would soon explode right onto him.

For him. Because of him.

She did not want to let him have the power over her that she knew he felt he deserved.

"Who am I to you?" He said again as he trailed a long lick from the front of her chuff, leading right down to her forbidden entrance - and waited impatiently.

Fuck it she would tell him!

"Rhys, you are Rhys." She cried as she reached the peak of coming, in which he stopped licking to taunt her yet again.

He stopped and muttered, "No, I am not. I am something else. Something more, not something less."

For fuck sake why must he be this way, she cried internally as she twitched in hungry eagerness! Why couldn't she come all over his chiselled, hungry face and be on her way out of there?

Be free.

Away from the darkness, and away from him. This beast…

Then as he scowled some more she twigged at his roaring words and groaned.

Must she really say it? But she guessed that if she wanted this ecstasy to continue on and on, to reach her peak, then she sadly must.

"My mate Rhys, you are my fated mate. My one and only."

"That`s better." He grinned mischievously. Sucking her perfect clit between his lips as she finally reached her peak and exploded all over his eager face.

He stood back up just as though he had not been munching her in her most delicate of places.

"And you were worrying about the volcano erupting..." Smirking.

"Haha. Can I have my knickers back?" She asked.

"No. They have my name on them now as you now do."

"Hmm! Suit yourself. Enjoy wearing them. Though looking at your thick muscular thighs I doubt you would get even one leg into them!" She sniggered but also secretly admired her man's large but toned legs.

The size difference between them was just so unreal. He was tall and huge; she was tall and willowy. Just as she liked it.

Now that she had finished being eaten alive by the master of the darkness she was starting to feel a bit out of place.

He smirked, "Wearing them? No, I will be sleeping with them as you your self will be soon for all of eternity." He took a hold of the knickers as though they were his most treasured item besides her and put them straight into his pocket.

"Very full of yourself aren't you? What, do you sleep in a coffin or something?" She teased. But thinking he likely did. He would hardly be the sort to have silk sheets. He probably lived in some kind of torture chamber!

He didn't hesitate, "No."

It was her turn to raise a mocking dark blonde brow at his candid answer, "Now that does surprise me! I could imagine you in a black, shiny coffin full of spiders and other scuttling insects to keep you company. Possibly a few worms. I hear they like the dead and you sir are old."

Centuries old.

She was surprised that he didn't disintegrate when he bent down to service her oh so very nicely that she squealed. She walked away, to get away, and he forcefully pulled her to him then reached over and his rough lips met hers.

"A lot of things would surprise you about me," He almost hissed into her stunned face. "And I don't need mere bugs to keep me company when I have the most annoying but still the most beautiful mate in the world. What more could a vamp like me need?"

"Take out?" She jested, "Cake? I hear you, but me and you would be a bad idea. I Can't stay here. You must know that by now Rhys?"

It was difficult when half of you wanted to run away kicking and screaming and to never return. But the other half was so desperate for you to stay exactly where you were, exactly who you should be with for all of time. But then if you did stay, was it worth the risk to get trapped in that god awful place until the end of your days?

No, no it was not. Anywhere would be better then there.

"Perhaps. Look Rhys, it was fun while it lasted. Haven't you got to go unfreeze your brother so that you can do ghastly deeds to him? You seem to enjoy them."

"That I do my dear, that I do. Now I am off to as you say do ghastly deeds to dear old Iden. You can either go wait in the castle or little old Ruby who is waiting inside will burn to ashes."

"You know the way to a girls heart don't you?" She sighed. "Ok, deal. Ruby much as I find her an interfering, annoying windbag doesn't deserve to be here."

He ran a clawed finger over her cheek, and she swore that she could see a smile trying to work its way out of his stern mouth as he bid her fair well for a time.

"Do as you are told. I expect to see you in there my Justina or else suffer the consequences."

She looked at him before he left. Nerves ran through her. "You would hurt your own mate? Me?"

Rhys bit his lip, "Never." He said very quietly growling under his breath but that she heard with her sharp vampire hearing.

Did he know that?

He spectacularly ran off, unleashing his glorious bat like wings while she tried not to stop and stare in complete and utter awe at his marvellous form.

Nobody, but nobody that she had ever seen but he had wings that looked like that. Trust a man, ok vamp like that to want to be different!

Born different.

She neared the castle again and pried open the door with a grip of the hand. Trying not to glance over at where her evil mate had taken advantage of her next to the castle wall. Why else would she have let him do that?

She traipsed through the castle. It was so big that if she was not careful she would surely get lost in there.

"Hello?" she called over and over. Wiping dusty cobwebs from her hanging blonde hair and hoping to god that there was no spiders in them because she would simply scream.

She might be now an immortal, but even she was scared of big hairy spiders!

Had he not heard of a thing known as a cleaner? No, it appeared not looking around at all the dust and eeriness that the place held in it. Could have at least used his dark magic for something!

She heard a scuttle behind her.

"Who, whose there?" She asked. Now she was jittery.

"Justina." A tiny whisper.

She edged forwards. Was it Ruby? It had better be.

It could be no one else. If it was another she vampire then she would claw her eyes out and lob them at her.

Rhys was hers.

"Ruby?" She called out warily, "Is that you?"

"Oh, it's you." It was her. Ruby finally reached her with a firm scowl that marred her small delicate face. She seemed what Justina could see to be gripping her hand as though she were hurt in some way.

Justina tried to see her hand, but Ruby noticed and so kept it hidden away.

"Don't look to pleased."

Tempted to up and out of there. She had better things to do. This was not one of them.

"I'm not. Are you here to rescue me?" Ruby looked slightly suspicious as she looked around in case it were a trap. For they hardly been best mates had they before this.

No, definitely not.

"It's complicated…"

"Complicated."

"Yes."

"It would be with you." Snapped Ruby. "It always is." Justina looked over at the smaller vamp who appeared so fucking fragile and who appeared to look weak as though a gust of wind could knock them over. She shouldn't care what the girl thought, but she strangely felt a bit hurt by the hostility that flowed out of the other female straight towards her.

"Did he do this?" She dared to ask Ruby as she finally spotted the charred hand dangling from behind her small formed back. Remembering Rhys's earlier threat of burning her if she did not get her arse into the castle it was obviously one of his favourite forms of torture.

Ruby only nodded and looked down at the charring that ran from her knuckles up to her lower wrist..

"He would do the same to you if he caught you here." Ruby warned.

Justina shuffled awkwardly on the spot. "Well, no he wouldn't. He made me come in here."

"Why?"

"It doesn't matter. Come. You need blood."

"That I do." Ruby sighed and licked her lips at the thought of it. Feeling the ravenous hunger eating her up from the inside. She followed Justina, ambling weakly behind her and not liking the difference in strength between them one bit.

After a few false leads and dead ends, they finally reached a kitchen with a huge fuck off fridge. Justina trotted over to it without delay, opening it.

It was full to the brim with blood.

Blood, blood and yes, more blood. More than the eye could see. More than one could ever need.

Poor Ruby had clearly been deprived of it when he had a whole massive fridge full of it!

How was that fair?

It wasn't. It really wasn't.

Justina grabbed a shit ton load of vials, the more the better and passed some quickly to Ruby before she passed out onto the ground. But before she could say anything else, Ruby had snatched some from her and was guzzling the sweet nectar down in one mouthful.

As though it was her first taste of blood.

Her fangs shooting out, her tongue ready to collect every last drop.

Nothing were said they both just drank their blood in peace. Ruby in extreme thirst and Justina due to her stress levels making her thirst oh so very much for it even more.

And then – truth time. It needed to be said out loud.

"He is my mate. Rhys I mean. He is my mate." Justina stood and waited now sated from the blood that flowed. Waiting for a reaction. Some kind of response.

Anything.

Ruby threw the bottle that she was drinking down smashing it and just stared open eyed as the glass surrounded her in tiny pieces.

"Say something. Please." Justina begged. "Anything."
She did not quite know why she begged, why she
cared, but she did. She needed an answer.

"Are you pleased about this?" A pause.

Was she? She guessed she should be. "Fifty, fifty." That
seemed like a good enough answer.

Ruby's blue eyes which were now changing to red
flickered over to hers in an instant.

"He is a cunt, but I do understand. It is what you hear
when you become one of the undead. You get your
own mate, the one fated to you and only you. Mine is
out there somewhere as well. I can`t wait to meet her.
For her to be mine whoever she is."

"She?" Then, "Oh yeah I remember you saying that."
Justina had forgotten the sexual revelation from before
Ruby was rudely kidnapped from their home.

Ruby tried to explain, "I wasn't trying to steal your
guy. Well, I was, but for my sister. I smelled that she
was his mate. Kinda weird but there you go."

"Oh. Sorry then. Do I smell like Rhys?" She wondered.
Shuddering at the thought of his masculine smell that
smelt like sheer power.

The power that her mate had over her.

Ruby winced and then leaned forward her elbows propped up, her hand still uglily charred. "To be honest? No. But then I assume the darkness has hidden that part of him. Either that or it was a fluke that I guessed Iden and Elfina being mates."

"Perhaps. But I think not. Let me look at your hand. Did you put it under water?" Justina fussed, reaching out with a look of concern.

"Yes. Its fucked. He fucked it. I never knew that you would have a caring side Justina."

Justina continued. "I do. I don't know why I am telling you this but here we are. Sit." They both plonked themselves onto the kitchen bar stools that surrounded a breakfast bar. Justina made them some tea and then began her tale.

"Before I died, I was a nurse. Just qualified but still a nurse. My dream job."

Ruby gasped as Justina continued. "I bloody loved it! No one thought that would be what I went into, judging me for the way that they thought I were. But I wanted to prove that I was more than just a pretty face. And prove it I so did when I graduated with a nursing degree." Ruby gasped again for good measure.

Then the sad part of the tale, the one that hurt like a thousand needles, "Then a few months later, Fess came along and took all that hard work away from me and everything that I had dreamed of. All because he wanted my body. My looks. Not me, just them. So that is why I enjoy soul collecting. It gives me a purpose that I needed. That I need. And I wouldn't want it any other way."

"I enjoy it too." The smaller vamp whispered in agreement.

Justina neared holding out a hand. An olive branch if you were. "I think I misjudged you then Ruby. Now let me look at that hand. Please. It might be too damaged beyond repair, but I can try to help even just the slightest. And then let's get you out of here.

CHAPTER FIVE

Then

Justina left the Norfolk Hospital with a tired grin on her sweet stunning face.

But still a grin none the less. The day had been so tyring. But nursing was a tyring job, wasn`t it? The past few months had been simply an amazing and exciting blur as she carefully settled into her new role as a fully qualified nurse at last with her own work load.

Her own patients. From the old to the new adults. The lovely ones to the hard work ones that cried and pushed the buzzer every five minutes and drove her to silent distraction.

And with people to rely on her.

The hospital nearest to her home sure, but one that she had spent her last placement working at through the UEA doing her degree. Putting her head down and getting on with it in the best way possible.

She sensed that good things were about to happen for her. She deserved them to.

She giggled out loud that one of the doctors that she had had her eye on had finally slipped her his number in their shared break. Which for once had coincided with each other's. Having worried that she had imagined the lingering looks and wide-eyed smiles that he had given her once or twice when he thought that she wasn't looking.

Feeling giddy as butterflies tore through her at the thought of him and what he had done. She may be biting the bullet, but they would have some fucking good-looking kids. He seemed to have a naughty streak as well when he was out of work that gave him an edge.

Her kind of guy.

Her future was looking up. A degree, new job, and a date with an actual doctor! Soon she would be looking for a new home too to complete things. Life was just great.

Then she heard it – a snigger. A shuffle and branches snapping. Footsteps approaching.

A warning alarm now blaring in her brain.

"Why hello there pretty lady." She turned around feeling slightly nervous at this because she was alone and it was dark, now 9pm and her good mood shifted in to something else.

Fear.

The hairs on the back of her neck stood up, goosebumps appeared on her lean arms, peeping out from beneath her nurses uniform.

No one was there. She appeared to be alone but clearly - wasn't.

She was now away from the hospital after being caught for a while in her own whirling thought bubble and now wishing that she had stayed back there and caught a bus to her home not but a few streets away. Why, oh why oh why!

She tried to walk quicker but something, no someone grabbed her harshly in a maddened grip.

"Get off!"

There was no one there.

It was like she was fighting an invisible force. Scared did not even come close to how she was feeling.

"You are coming with me." The voice said again. She tried to fight back, she kicked, slapped, elbowed the air with no one there.

"Where are you?" panic ally asking.

"Here. Don`t be frightened, it will all be over soon." Then a mad chuckle. She kicked out again, still seeing no one but fearing someone anyway, and managed to run away for a time. Passing a bush, she then stumbled in her short, smart shoes onto her spread out hands.

And landed next to a pile of corpses peeping out from behind the large thorny bush. She screamed loudly and was grabbed roughly again.

Fingers pinching her skin.

"Who are you? Why can I not see you? Am I going to be like them?" She pointed with a shaky finger at the corpses that lay on the floor, hidden so that only she could see.

Trying to break free.

Retching at the blood and the flies buzzing around hungry for a meal. The one nearest looked as though it had been savagely bitten in all manner of places.

Who was this monster? She still could not see him. Feel him? Yes, in every way.

A whisper in her ear. A stinking breath.

"Oh, no darlin. Don't be frightened, because I have more planned for you." Then a bite to her neck and it all went scarily black.

She arose sometime later in some kind of bright white building. Simply beautiful. Pillars, statues, and lots of desks in between.

Desks? And lots of small people pottering about all over the place…

Was she dreaming? No, it appeared not as she was grabbed off the floor again. But lighter this time.

Hunger whirled around her, and she wanted to strangely devour every person who was in near sight.

"Now, now." That voice again whispered in a croaky way. She glanced. What! She could see him now. Tall, muscled, blonde hair in whisps. His face smiling but beyond it looked only badness.

She flinched at the contact. "Behave in here. One wrong bite and they will put you down like a dog. Understand?" She nodded meekly. Wondering how he knew that she wanted to bite people, and how she got here wherever here were.

Every ounce of strength had long left her.

Then she saw them. Ghosts milling around. Some alone and others with what appeared to be people. Normal sized ones. This was not happening; she was scared out of her damn mind!

As she shook in fear she asked the question that was on her nervous lips, "Who are you? Why am I so hungry for…?"

"Shh." The blonde evil handsome one who frightened her muttered. "It's our turn for check in. Remember to behave."

She was prodded forwards towards a desk and sat down in the chair. Everything hurt, she felt weird. The small lady with the bob gestured her over. A lady that she wanted to eat so very desperately until there was just bones.

What the hell was happening? She had thought he was going to use her, kill her, but she was still here. Not quite here but not quite there.

And that was just the start of it.

The beginning of her immortal life.

CHAPTER SIX

Rhys

He had thrown the teenagers soul into the judgment court for them to deal with instead of he. Feeling dirty that that drug addled teen had been picked up by him and he had then carried it in his muscular arms there to be judged by them that worked there.

But knowing that even if he had wanted to that he sadly had to treat all the souls he collected the same way. He didn't have to like it, but as long as he didn't voice it at all for others had been ended for not complying.

But the dirty scrote had still tasted unbelievably good! His blood now belonged to him and him alone. He would not waste his own powerful one on that kid in return though. For he did not deserve to live again. He hadn't died with drugs running through him no, for even he would have not touched the blood if he had.

But a shootout among foes had gone horribly wrong and had ended him. And now the soul would soon be elsewhere.

Probably the lower plains. Rhys did not care where the boy ended up as long as he was not with him, and he never had to see his simpering wet soul again!

He rarely did not care. In his opinion it was natural selection at its best. He himself did not enjoy living either, not any more. Hadn't in centuries. Each year becoming a simple replica of the last.

But he was determined to stay alive to wait for his own one to come to him.

Something that belonged to him and only him.

Something that no one could take away. Would she be as bad as him? Or meek, soft, sweet, and innocent that he could mould her into how he saw fit?

Who would get on her knees whenever he told her to and take what she could from his dripping large cock as he forced it between her lips until she screamed.

He churned with desire at what would one day come his way. An erection building in his tight outfit.

He now after leaving a crack in the wall, a crack that felt like it gave the big building some character after all these years, he felt like he was being watched. But then his paranoia was up there with his rage that he liked to unleash on unsuspecting people without delay.

Hmm. He was not sure. If they were there then they were hiding well from him. He did not like that thought though. Not liking being outwitted.

Why were they watching him and what the heck did they want? His large hand flexed at the thought of smacking something hard.

He leapt into the air. As he flew through the sky back towards the darkness, his sanctuary, a smell washed over him. Like the way that annoying Ruby had smelled but so much better.

It reminded him of home from a long time ago. As he landed he looked around. Over here, over there and upwards. Then he looked behind.

And that was when he saw her. A beauty with wide eyes, a slim body like that of a curvy model. A slim waist that led to slightly jutting out hips. Fangs like he, and blonde flowing hair like a summers day that blowed in the wind.

Could it be? he mused as he studied her briefly. No, it must be some kind of trick.

It must! For he had scoured the human world for years upon years, searching for his mate. The one to call his.

And she was here in his world all along! Just not of the dark part but there of the light. She was the light, and he was the... well you know!

"What trickery is this?" He groaned throatily as he impatiently threw her to him with a blast of something extra that he had conjured up.

Dark delicious magic.

Now that she was gripped in his dark gaze. She was stuck there. Not by magic but by the connection that they both felt inside their eternal souls. The wanting, the needing...

"Who are you to come here into my domain with all your precious beauty, and then leave me? How dare you even try!" He cursed. He would not let her go now that he had found her after all these years. He would not! He would chain her to him if he could. Feel the power that her skin next to his would create.

Enjoy the sound of her moans as she sucked his cock hard as if she owned it. Which she would. She already did. She could have it.

He ran a finger through her golden hair, wanting a part of her near for all eternity. So, light compared to his own he found, but still so darn perfect. Her skin pale like his he knew that they would both be a force to be reckoned with.

She appeared frightened by him. Strangely he did not like this. He wanted to touch her, lick her, caress her all over until her body hummed next to his. To dominate while she submitted. After all wasn't that what a mate was for?

And then bloody Iden and Elfina came for that damn annoying whimpering Ruby.

Ruining everything that he had pushed towards! Thankfully as Fess came out of nowhere with a sharp demanding growl, sweeping the stunned blood starved newbie vamp off her feet he ordered his one to go to the castle and wait for him.

He wouldn't be long, they had years to catch up on, so they did. But first he would freeze his brother temporarily, make him stew and learn his lesson. He wouldn't kill him, no not yet though he was tempted to.

Ninety-nine percent of him wanted to blow his brother into kingdom come. He was his brother, he had sired him but this toing and froing, the rage felt between them, the endless fighting... he would not let that get in the way of being with his Justina.

Her name sung like glory.

He knew deep in his darkened heart that as serious as she tried to pretend that she were that she would not forgive him for killing her clan leader. Even though the fact that they had fucked and more than once, would take him a long time to wipe from his addled mind!

His sweetheart with his own brother! Enraged he shot out an invisible weapon and hit Iden hard as he could and then hit him in the nuts with a well-placed knee that made him wince and drop to his knees.

Where he belonged.

"Coward!" Iden cried. "Cheat! A gentleman knows not to hit another one in the restricted area!"

"I am hardly no gentleman." Rhys himself spat back as he rose to hit him again. His fist ready to plummet him into next week. He would ensure that he could not soul collect for a time.

Their glorious wings both shot out as they danced and fought. Iden's more angel like next to Rhys bat like ones. The two brothers looking so alike but then oh so very different as well.

As Iden took out his marvellous sword and held it to Rhys neck, his brother knocked him back and they both spiralled to the ground in a daze. The power between them near enough equal, but the dark ones all the more due to him having the upper hand.

Dark magic. Turning his brother into a living statue while he went to seek out his mate. Not liking that she had been away from him if only for a few short minutes.

It was too much! She was his! Curse his brother and his snidey interference. See how he liked being frozen and unable to move while his mate was taken from him.

Rhys looked at Iden and laughed evilly. Was that his imagination or did the younger one scowl? No, he must be mistaken for he was well and truly frozen.

Pity the magic was not permanent.

Glancing back briefly he then made his way forward with long strides towards his castle. Dark, dangerous but magnificent. He knew that he would have to let Justina work her magic in order for her to stay there.

But he would force her anyway. Like he would be tempted to do with his cock when he next saw her. Get her on her knees like he had thought about so many times before they met.

Though he would not need to as he smelt the desire that ran off of her pussy.

The one that would be his undoing.

There she was.

Still plucking up the courage to make her way into his glorious home which was now in part - also hers. He jumped out causing a gasp to come from her delectable plump lips.

As he taunted and teased her and got her to take her knickers off for him, causing a blush to come over her fair cheeks - something came over him.

Adoration. He didn't want his mate to be scared of him. He wanted her to love him, want him and most importantly - he wanted her to adore him too.

He now no longer wanted to push her onto her knees making her take his impressive cock in his mouth, making her weep, begging him to stop until she choked on his spunk.

No.

He did not want to hurt a hair on her pretty fair head, and he would decapitate anyone who tried to. Now he wanted her to sing for him. Now he wanted to eat her sweet-smelling pussy, watch, and feel and lick, and finger it with retracted claws until he became her undoing.

Him. He loved it! So, he did that. She gasped again as he settled between her thighs – and got to work.

The castle was no longer his home, this pussy was.

She was.

CHAPTER SEVEN

"Thank you for telling me your story." Ruby said wiping a tear from her eyes as they tidied up the blood vials that they had both devoured hungrily.

Even vampires cried. They were dead not emotionless!

"I`m sorry for getting arsey with you when you interrupted me and Iden before. It was not very nice of me." Justina tried to explain.

"It's ok."

"No, it's not." Justina shook her head. Regretting that she had treated young Ruby like merely shit that was on her shoe, for no reason at all. She would change, she would. No longer wanting to act hardened so that others didn't walk over her no longer.

To be herself.

With him. Was that even possible? It should be for the fates didn't lie.

"Can I ask you your story?"

"It's grim." Said Ruby in reply. Not liking to talk of it. Ever.

Her lips stiffening. Eyes clearly troubled by what had happened to cause her to become the living dead.

"It can't be any worse than mine! Taken after work for some shady vampire harem." Justina tried to make a joke of it. But the thing was, it would haunt her every day from then on in. Every day that she lived was a day that she was not doing her role.

Her nursing one. The one that she had strived so hard for. Couldn't she have just had a little bit longer alive? It was taken from her too soon.

Ruby sprang her white wings out and cocooned them around herself. Keeping her feeling safe in her own personal haven. "It's not a competition, but if you can call being beaten to within an inch of my life on the way home from a night out and then sexually assaulted by four sick individuals, which eventually led to my death..."

The thud of footsteps came from behind them as they divulged their darkest fears to the other one.

Both their dead hearts dropped into their chests at the sound coming towards them. Rubys now from immortalising fear, and Justinas from fear for the other vamp stood beside her.

And desire. Cos he smelled so good… That was one good thing that she could say about her mate!

Then a rough voice came from behind. With words that no one, but no one in the whole and entire realm would expect to ever be spoken a loud.

But they were.

"Who?" Rhy`s eyes turned blood red in absolute anger. Almost glowing.

"What do you mean?" Justina dared asked as he seethed on the spot about things unknown. Feigning ignorance to his question. It was better that way.

Dismissing her softly he said, "Not you my fated one. Her." He pointed straight at Ruby whose eyes bulged in surprise at the question by someone so possibly evil that she would not expect that he even cared. "Who did that to you?"

"The assault? The rest?" She said in response to him.

"Yes." Rhys almost seethed with venom.

Looking like a mad man, but neither of the women were no longer scared of him now. He was too busy getting wound up by other monsters doings.

He was the only monster around. Only he!

Ruby fiddled nervously with her fingers as she spoke, "They are five years dead. Iden and I went down to Earth a few months later and tore out their throats in a mad blood bath. But why should you care? Look what you did to my hand! You kept me here even after you found out that I wasn't your true mate. Even after you found your real one I was still here. That was not fair, nor was it right."

He looked over at Justina who merely shrugged, "She's right Hun."

Rhys backed off. "Good. I am glad that they are dead then. If they were not then they soon would be at my hand."

"Like you yourself deserve to be! And our hand? What of my hand? God damn it look at my hand you absolute bloody creatin!" Ruby showed her charred hand for all in attendance to witness.

The one that would never heal. He had done that to her! The fucking monster!

"I might have gone a bit over board there…" Not quite an apology but the best they would get.
"A bit! A bit!" Ruby screeched outraged. Justina tried to reassure her. Glowering at her fated one.

"You cannot compare me to rapists! I might be hot headed but that I am not. Now…" He strode forward and put a possessive arm around Justina. "You can leave." Turning to Ruby.

Holding his fated one close, sniffing her hair and rubbing her arms. Not holding up, not letting go.

"Leave?" A whimper fled the small women's lips.

"Yes." He nodded slowly. "You have ten minutes to leave the castle. If you are still in my line of sight then, then you will stay here forever as a prisoner. Regardless of what my Justina says…But I want something in exchange from you for it." He paused then glowered. "Or shall I say some one…" Eyes narrowing.

The two women looked at him in surprise.

"Let me guess. Me?" Justina whispered. Her gut churned at the thought of being made to stay in that horrible place.

For all her immortal years.

"Who else would I want?" Rhys grinned mischievously.

"Deal. Now go." Nodded Justina. Stepping forward and gently pushing Ruby towards the door. Not wanting to stay, but not wanting poor Ruby to be stuck there either. Maybe the place with all its doom, destruction and misery would finally grow on her. And if it did not then that was a risk she was willing to take to earn the other women's freedom.

Ruby stumbled off and presumably left the castle for elsewhere. No doubt excited to get out of there. Hurrying before the force field got reactivated and she were stuck there.

"Where is your brother? Elfina?"

"Why?" A snarl as anticipated by him.

"And Fess? Will he be back here?" She wondered aloud. Hoping not. Praying not either.

Rhys growled at the mere mentions of other men near his woman. Soon he would have to claim her, for if it took much longer then his cock would literally spring from his pants and plunge straight in…

His grip grew rougher.

"Ow, just fuck off Rhys!"

"No." He spat back viciously with venom. "Why all the questions I ask?"

"Iden is my clan leader, Elfina is a baby vamp who has been taken. I feel sympathy towards her. I am just trying to help them. And Fess is… Fess is…" She stuttered.

"Fess is what?" A hiss. Clanging of teeth.

"It doesn't matter. Not now."

"It does to me as it seems to you."

She sighed; He wouldn't let the matter drop would he? "Fess is my sire. I am one of the group of women he savagely turned into vamps for his own pleasure."

He to her surprise took her hand with his own. His expression went from ice fire to warm, comforting heat that she needed.

It was as if he yearned for her but also wanted to comfort her, protect her – keep her safe.

"I never realised." He said gently as his eyes bored straight into hers. Brushing a hair from her forehead so that he could see her better.

Hear her better. Eat her better perhaps…

"I think he changed since then. But I still hate him with a passion. He stole everything from me!" Now her own eyes were glowing red in warning to the one who had caused what she had been through.

"Did he hurt you?" He growled with a snarl in her ear. Not letting go of her hand even for an instant though he was truly tempted to. In order to lose his shit, trash the place, send Fess to the lower plains, and watch him burn!

But instead, he chose to comfort his obviously upset mate as tears threatened to drop onto the ground.

"No. Only when he turned me." She whispered. "But after we all rejected him, and your brother banished him then I never saw him again. I thought he had been killed! Until today that is, when he whipped Elfina away from here to who knows the fuck where."

"You don't have to worry about him now my beautiful mate." Rhys laid a kiss on her that almost melted his dead heart. "He will soon enough. No one, but no one fucks me over! And especially not to my mate either! How dare he! He will die for this. In pain for his greed."

"And I will enjoy watching it." She said with a wicked grin. Her goodness rubbing off on him, but now it appeared that his dark side was rubbing off onto her!

CHAPTER EIGHT

He showed her to his magnificent crypt where all his favourite glorious things laid. The artifacts that he had collected over the years as a fearless immortal, to keep away the boredom.

There were so many that they were not all kept there. But the ones that meant something - did.

The bed that lay in the middle of it for him to take his future bride. No coffin for him, for he were not dead yet.

Not quite.

The sheets were black silk and soft. He instantly with a growl pushed his one gently down onto the bed fully clothed, and kissed her hard, his stubble brushing her pale cheek as his wanting lips met hers.

She stifled a moan as the kiss became a tangle of tongues. His was oddly pierced. What could that tongue do when it met somewhere sweet and wet?

She could feel the heat powering down to her crotch at the thought of it, and as they kissed, and he gave himself to her the heat moved to her stone-cold heart. This man had more light in him then he ever realised.

"I'm not sure I'm ready." She said honestly. For things were moving too fast that her mind spun.

Her head was in two minds about what direction it wanted her to go now.

He let his hair down loose as she looked on in awe at him. Still hot stuff. Shrugging, "We will take as long as it takes, but just know that I am not a patient man, my one. I will take you and when I do you will belong with me, to me, by me. Especially for me." This was said with one of his growls that fired her soul up until it almost caught fire.

She struggled to speak; her words caught in her swollen chest. That statement had nearly brought her down. Nearly stopped her from wanting to break free from this awful castle.

Sneak off in the dead of night never to be found again.

"I don't know whether this thing, you, and I will work."

He frowned, "It is written in destiny. Why wouldn't it? Do you think that I would hurt you in any way?" He then softened. "I have never felt this vulnerable since meeting you. Ever. If you got hurt it could send me to complete and utter madness that could knock down my kingdom!"

"Oh Rhys!" She cried. Was this really true?

She could love him, badness or not, and all else besides. She could lust after him. But she had not wanted to lose her heart to him and for he to take it away from her. She herself was also vulnerable to the bond that they now shared.

Every touch, every kiss, every word made her throat swell up with undiluted happiness that threatened to burst out of her. She never thought that she would get here, to this point in time, but her monster had proved her otherwise.

"What?" He asked, frowning again.

Surprised by her outburst. Surprised that it filled him with some kind of strange warmth unlike none he had felt before. The fists that he used for punching, breaking and destruction were now used to pull his one tight to him as he kissed her more gently this time.

"I feel the same my Rhys. And with all the darkness that swirls around you, it is likely that you will meet your sad end way before I."

"That may be, but at least I have known you."

Happiness cursed her soul alike no other now. She had everything she could want. Whenever she wanted it. She had never expected Rhys to be this honest. She never expected him to be the man she needed him to be.

Minus the nursing for there was little need for it in there world where a simple cut could shrunk in the blink of an eye. Only the more serious injuries took their time to heal. But with time she hoped the pain of losing her life, becoming something else, would hurt less over time until it no longer mattered at all.

Smiling broadly her long lashed eyes met his red ones.

He returned it in an instant, no hesitation involved. It was funny for the beauty like queen to see such a fierce beast such as he smiling so darn bright. But it made him all the more handsome. Like just a moment of light had eroded the darkness.

Just a moment but it was still there.

She tried to explain what she was feeling, "I want to be here; I just don't like the darkness. Its creepy as. Why can't our home be anywhere but here?"

"Oh. That is a problem." Rhys grimaced. "Eternals like us, like me and Fess the one who won`t be immortal much longer once I get my claws on him, we like it. It just takes getting used to. It is just you with your beauty… it will take longer to fit in here." Cupping her chin in his powerful grip as though she were some rare priceless treasure.

She gasped. Outrage hitting full force.

"My beauty! My beauty!" Justina screamed in his startled face as she pulled away. Ripping herself away. Feeling so stupid for being vulnerable with him.

Almost going nuclear. He looked at his little spit fire with surprise but also a hint of worry behind the unseen mask that he wore. An emotion that the bad one was not used to.

The master of the dark grabbed hold of her once more and looked straight into those piercing eyes as she whispered. "Is that all I am to you? Beauty? My beauty has been nothing but a curse to me. I wish I could give it away. I would rather be ugly then this."

"Never!" Rhys hissed. "You are my everything. I do not care if you look like the beauty you are, or like the beast in the books. You are mine Justina and mine alone and tell me you know you are so much more than that. Tell me, damn you!"

She quietened down. Now standing over him.

A knock at the door interrupted them from their heated moment. The first thing that bonded them.

It were Fess.

"Rhys could I speak to you please?" He asked through the locked door. A pause while he waited for some kind of answer from his master.

Rhys`s eyes nearly bulged out his head on hearing the man speak that had caused his mate so much grief that tears left her lids. Who had killed her shamelessly without thought. Who had unknowingly tormented her ever since.

Well, no more! Gone were the days when she would think herself just beauty. He would help her see that she were more than that. Her sires death would be the start…

As his mind raced he moved away from Justina and smashed his fist into a table hard making the wood crack. The shadows jumped but then took control again as they surrounded him.

They were at the beck and call of their master.

Only he could set them free.

"Calm down." She whispered on seeing the black swirling out of him, heading towards the door. Wishing they would leave. Reaching out and rubbing his neck, causing him to let out a stifled groan as his cock hardened at his mates touch. "Don't let on that you know. We will surprise him! Ok?"

She did not know how she would feel facing Fess for the first time in the years. It made her tremble with a nervous energy that would not yield. But she was now stronger than he.

And she had the darkness at her side. Sooner than later – in her.

What did Fess have? Nothing. That was what.

He needed to pay to what he did to all those women, by god he did! Justina knew. Some survived the ordeal that he bestowed on them and became like she, but others they did not survive. Their families deserved justice.

It was up to her to get revenge for them all. If Rhys wanted to do it on her behalf? Then so be it, she would let him go ape shit on her blonde torturer.

She would be proud of him. Her man, her roaring but secretly gentle mate who was hers to hold, to treasure, to tease and taunt for all eternity.

No longer hers to hate.

She would support his violence every step of the way. And she would enjoy watching it unfold.

"Give me ten and meet me outside." Rhys commanded.

"Of course, sir." Fess seemed to go away but seconds later came back and spoke through the door. "I have brought Elfina, she is in my quarters. Will you help keep her safe?"

Rhys pondered for a moment. Justina could almost see the cogs turning as he thought.

"Yes. Be on your way. I am busy."

"Oh. It's like that is it? You haven't had a women in a while. Enjoy!" A snigger. Not realising that the sound of his voice was sending the two in the crypt into a mad revenge filled frenzy.

The sound of footsteps let them know that he had thankfully gone. Sighs of reliefs all around.

Rhys looked at Justina with a small smile that did not reach his eyes.

"Shall we?"

She studied him for a moment. A scowl on her pretty face. "You haven't had a woman in a while?" She huffed. Gesturing snarkily at the woman part.

"Says the woman that was bedding my brother." Was snapped back.

Wow. She kind of was asking for that one...

"I didn't know he was your bloody brother!" she exclaimed, "I didn't know I had a monstrous mate somewhere out there!"

"And I did?"

He had a point she supposed. But she still huffed again anyway for good measure. "Any more woman from hereon in and I will skin you up, mate!"

He smirked knowingly, "Trust me mate, you are more than enough for me."

"Charming."

"I try to be." He grinned in retaliation. She still couldn't get over how someone as dark, depraved as him were – she had heard the stories, could be when his face lit up for her.

"Did anyone tell you how handsome you were when you actually smiled." She teased with awe in her eyes.

"No."

She pecked him on the cheek.

"That's surprising."

"Not really. I haven't smiled in years until I met you." He got up of the bed. Wishing he could lay her down and have her.

"Let's finish this." But before they made to leave, Justina spaced out – a badly timed soul call calling her.

She shook herself free from her trance. Her mate just holding her waiting for it to pass. Not interrupting it – he couldn't, and it was a private time for a vamp which one should abide to. Even though he himself hated them.

"I got to go." The soul needed her. Twitching awkwardly not knowing how he would react when she went.

"You had better come back." He said. His face hardening again, the soft man she had seen now appeared gone.

"Yes. But Fess better have been dealt with by then. Promise me that." She did not want to see him again, she couldn't. She did not know what to do if she did…

He nodded then threw himself out the door. Showing her his trust that she would return- so she took his trust and left too. Missing him already.

Her opinion of him now long changed

CHAPTER NINE

The body Justina was called to collect belonged to a large man who had it seemed eaten himself to death. His stomach not just round but a mass of loose flesh that hanged down towards his popped-up trousers.

Before this day the sight of him may have caused her to wrinkle her nose and hide her disgust at the smell and the sight in that food filled flat. But something had changed in her that day.

All she felt was pity for him. He appeared to be alone, died alone with just the comfort of his food. No one deserved that fate.

No one.

As he took his last gasp of breath in the human world, she eagerly sunk her fangs into his wrist. Chowing down on his delicious tasting blood. Feeling the calm that went through her as his blood became hers. When she was fully satisfied, her power restoring and there was no more blood left for anyone to have, she carefully picked the soul up that had now detached from its crumpled body and took it on its way.

To its final destination. Hoping that he would find some peace as he made his last step.

Much stronger than a human she could lift many things. But the human soul was light to the touch and did not bare any weight. There was no struggle as she tore through the grotty flat with him now in her arms.

Wings unleashing for nobody to see. For she was invisible, there would be no trace of her having being there.

In cases like this that was how it was better to be.

Meanwhile Rhys was facing off to the enemy.

"Rhys what's wrong?" Fess asked as the king of the darkness stared at him silently. His eyebrow shot up in question. Appearing to have no idea what he had done. No idea at all. He was soon to find out...

"Did you know?" Rhys snarled.

"Did I know what?"

"You know what!" Pushing Fess hard until he tumbled to the ground. Claws around his neck. His strength was a hundred times what the younger vamps were even without the magic that he stole.

Fess`s eyes bulged, "Hey man I haven't done anything wrong! What do you think you are doing!" He got up and with a roar and a charge that no one could have expected, he grabbed Rhys and pushed him right back.

"My mate. Do you know who my mate is?" A howl as the dark ones emotions poured out for all but him to see.

Fess wrinkled his nose.

Unsure. It appeared he did not know after all. "No. You found her? Congratulations! Elfina has two, did you know that?"

"No one has two you stupid fool Fess!"

"Elfina does. We saw…I mean we heard…"

"No one has two mates." The thought of Justina having two mates would have killed him off. But he knew the rules. One vampire and one human mate. Unless they had already been turned of course.

Not two. One.

Adding to the slow reacting blonde moron, "Justina. My mate is Justina. You turned her for your fucking stupid harem! It is lucky that she didn't sleep with you as I would have killed you even quicker. Now you are going to die. I am going to be the one to kill you."

Fess gulped. You could see in his eyes that he was desperately wondering how to get out of this. Eyes darting each way for a way to escape this.

Rhys grabbed him pushing him down, pounding the other vamps head down over and over again until he eventually passed out.

He stood waiting over the injured vamp. Waiting for him to rise again, to heal. Then he was going to do it over and over again.

Fess groaned from on the floor and tried to stand up.

"Why didn't you just finish the job?"

"Oh no my Fess. We are just getting started here."

"I swear man I did not know who she was!" Panting.

"It doesn't matter! Everyone even a monster like me knows that you get a women's consent before you do anything. You my friend didn't. You killed her! She was mine to kill! Mine!"

The dark master with his black swirls going wild took a hold of Fess. His palm flickered with dark magic; eyes even darker red as his power increased tenth fold.

A shock went into Fess.

He flew across the darkened ground as if he had been struck by a bolt of lightning. Sparks lit the ground. Scorch marks charred his fair skin.

Rhys stood on the blondes back so that he could not rise from the floor where he lay.

Not yet. Not until he wanted him to.

The sound of wings flapping gently, someone landing nearby. To watch? Or to help Fess? It appeared it was the first one.

"Don't let me stop you brother."

Iden was back. And he were alone. His long leather jacket flapping in the breeze as he took in the sight of his maddened enraged brother and his former clan mate.

"Oh, you won't." Rhys sneered.

"I am not the enemy here." An invisible olive branch was handed over. Would the other take it?

"No. You are not for once. Want to join in for old times' sake?" Rhys appeared to be relishing in Fess`s down fall. Sneering at it.

Iden had better things to do. "Nah. I need to find my mate. I take it she is here?" He asked.

"That she is."

"Thank you. Here... take this." Iden threw a vial of fresh blood at his brother who straight away caught it in the palm of his hands. "A- . Your favourite if I recall brother."

"That it is." His brother still knew him so well. He wondered what blood type Justina were? Although it would not have the sweet zing of human blood, he bet she tasted like sheer bliss.

"She's mine. Damn you!" Fess hollered twitching from under Rhys`s firm boot. Eyes blaring red as he tried and failed to put up a fight come what may. But didn't he know that no one, but no one messed with ones mate and got away with it!

Rhys would enjoy watching him burn. Watching him become- nothing.

"He was waffling about Elfina having two mates." Rhys explained at the annoyance wriggling like a squirming maggot under foot. Knowing that these words would send his usually cool brother into a spin.

And in three, two, one - It worked...

Iden stormed over in a craze, kicking Fess hard in the head. Fess`s neck snapped back sending him into a forced slumber once more. His elder tutted at the fact he would have to wait for his victim to awaken before he started on him again.

Even he wouldn't kick someone who was unconscious. He liked a fight. Liked being told what a scum bag he were.

Because he was.

"Two mates." Iden muttered in disbelief that anyone would be foolish enough to believe a thing. Muttering, "Imbecile." Heading off towards the castle with a swagger as he left his ex-clan mate to his fate.

"Remember to keep away from my mate." Rhys warned him before he faded into the distance.

"I have my own."

"Still…"

Iden stopped then traced his steps back. Eying his brother warily as if he had something he wanted to say. "How do you seal the bond if she is already… you know? Dead?"

"That I don't know." Because he had not heard of a human mate being already a vamp.

"I suppose if you swap blood then it may still work?"

"Perhaps. She is mine with or without the sacred blood bond." Rhys fiercely insisted.

"True but…"

"Oh, bugger off!" Rhys could see that Fess was opening his eyes again for round three. Iden scowled at this and walked steadily off.

His need for Elfina bigger then his need for revenge.

Fess appeared done. There was no fight in him left. Did he have any chance anyway?

No, not really.

"Look how long am I going to suffer this way? If you are going to finish me off, then for fucks sake just do it man!"

"As long as I feel…"

"But you don't feel Rhys. Maybe you should throw me into the volcano? It would be quicker!"

"Times change. And quick is not what you deserve."

"Maybe. I'm sorry for what I did sir. If only you knew why. You have no idea!"

"Frankly my dear Fess I no longer care. The only thing I care about is my precious princess. Oh, the one that you turned into a vampire just to get your limp tiny dick wet!"

"It wasn't that. It wasn't! You must believe me!"

Rhys`s monster was going bananas inside him, "Maybe so. You didn't even get it wet though did you? They all turned away, leaving you well and truly alone as you so deserve to be."

Fess grimaced, "That is all I am – alone. Even Elfina turned their head instead of me. They didn't see me…People don't know what I am, they don't know at all…" lowering his blonde head to as he now kneeled on the ground.

"Shut your pathetic waffling up. Now fuck off and die!" Flames licked the dark ones fingers and encased his large palms.

Fess closed his eyes – knowing what was coming to him and too afraid to fight it. He turned so the flames would keep off his front when the flames came calling. But he went up in a bundle of flames.

Screaming as he burned.

Trying and failing to put the flames out. Noone came to his aid.

Not even staying to join the show, Rhys turned laughing and walked off back towards his castle. His feelings for his mate calling his name.

As he entered he heard the sound of footsteps ahead of him. So, he held back and decided to eavesdrop instead. Tired from fighting he needed a rest. But by god, one move on his mate and whoever it were would be frankly… toast.

Like Fess now was…

CHAPTER TEN

Justina returned and secretly went towards the entrance on what was she supposed was her new home. She made sure not to get in the way of her rip-roaring mate and his amorous revenge plan.

She had wanted to watch, to join in. To See her sire, die horribly… but in the end she discovered that she just couldn't face it…face him.

"Now what room is yours Fess?" She said aloud to herself as she searched for his captive - Elfina. If she could not do something right by helping her man take down Fess, punish him, annihilate him, then she had decided that instead she would help the new vamp by setting her free from there.

Helping her to escape like she had done her sister.

Many doors later, some appearing familiar from when she searched the castle frantically with Ruby, others not.

"Fucking stupid castle." She muttered under her breath. Until she eventually found Fess`s room.

Even the outside of it gave her bad vibes. Skulls adorned the walls and the heads looked like they had died screaming in agonising pain.

It was locked. Typical!

She barged the door down in a fit of rage on then hearing crying coming from the other side of the thick door as she reached it.

As the door went to, Elfina was seemingly stunned to see the blonde beauty being the one to come to her rescue.

Out of all the rescuers she would have likely had, the one she at least expected was the one to help her!

"I'm here Elfina. I'm here." Justina said sweetly. Untying her from her binds and pulling her in for a surprising hug. The blonde comforting the smaller brunette.

"Thank you…" Elfina stuttered. She looked pale and weak. It appeared Fess had given her enough blood to come around when she collapsed, but not enough to regain her baby vamp strength so that she could break free from being chained to the bed.

Fess did either not want her to leave the room or he was as kinky as!

"Your welcome." Justina said. Walking over to the small fridge in the room and handed a vial of blood to Elfina who almost growled at seeing her lifeline handed to her for her to take. Feeling a sense of déjà vu as it was passed to her, Justina having not long done this with the woman`s smaller sister.

Waiting, watching, while Elfina downed it hungrily, almost weeping, and her eyes shot red from satisfaction.

"It is strange how good this stuff tastes now." Licking her lips. Elfina's skin went from a shade of grey to a more pasty colour. For she was dead after all.

"I know."

"And Fess?" Elfina asked. "Where is he?" She openly shuddered.

"I think he's dead." Justina reassured. " Rhys was plummeting him into the next realm when I discretely walked past so that I was not seen by either of them. I could not stomach it. Stomach him."

"Oh. Is it bad that I feel nothing?"

Both having more in common then they realised.

"Not really. I don't either. He is a bit of a cock. He turned me just to have something pretty there on his arm to hold. Now he likely has no arms."

Elfina surprisingly giggled at this. Justina joined in and they were both sniggering in the room with a mouth full of glorious blood when Iden walked in, followed shortly by Barren.

"You ok my beloved?" Iden said, wrapping his mate lovingly in his arms.

In his invisible hold.

"Well, you appear ok..." Raising a brow presumably at the fact that his new mate was laughing with Justina like they were old, trusted friends. When his mate was fully aware that he had slept with the model like creature.

Suppose it was better than rivals of course...

"We were just talking about Fess." Said Justina as Elfina stood and giddily gripped her mate back. Justina and Barren turned around not watching when their hug started to became like something out of a knock off soft porn film.

"Barren..."

"Justina..." He replied back too stunned for words.

"He let Ruby go in exchange for me." She explained to him, "I know you were fond of her. I mean you are fond of her. She's ok." Awkward smiling.

Barren breathed a sigh of relief at the fact that Ruby had broken free and left there.

"Oh brill! But for you? I don't understand."

"They are sadly for her, mates." Iden interrupted as he finally prised himself away from his new bride to be in order to speak to Barren.

"Ruby? You said he let her go?" Elfina appeared relieved. Still having not seen her sister since she had become immortal.

Would she ever?

"Yes."

"You let her go in exchange for you? I will never be able to thank you enough." Elfina cried out with joy.

"It`s fine really." Justina said. "For I know I am the only one that he will not hurt. But honestly, I don't know where she went, she just ambled off and got away from here. And the vampire realm is a big old place...much of it is not yet explored."

Barren was now busy rifling through the mini fridge and pulled some blood out to consume. Due to him having hot footed it there when his clan leader failed to return as quickly as he had hoped he would.

Which was not long. "We will find her." Handing a vial to Iden, the others shook their heads no.

 Pouring the blood down his throat – Barren then strangely gasped.

He went pale, coughing, gripping his throat. Then he just stood there in silence in total shock. Fear spread through his smouldering face.

A dark look came over him that nearly matched his dark hair.

"Is he ok?" Elfina asked Iden who was shaking Barren gently. Unable to rouse him from whatever had ailed him.

Truthfully? "No, I don't think he is."

"Poison?" Elfina asked paling.

"Where did he get this?" Barren snapped suddenly out of his sudden daze and grabbed hold of Justinas arm sharply. Gripping it with firm pointed claws and not letting go at all.

"The blood? Why? I don't know. Is it poisoned? Elfina and I were just tucking in also so…" Her stomach clenched at the thought of it. Looks passed between the two now fearful woman and Iden growled protectively at harm coming to his mate.

Barren shook his head, "No. No it is not. I said where did you get it?" There was an urgency there.

"Er… humans?" Elfina was also confused. Every vamp knew where they got their blood from! Humans or animals as a last resort. Preferring their feast on a human vein then a cute kitten.

Barren almost shattered, "But It's her! This is my mates blood. I saw a flash of blonde as I drank it with these very lips. Where did he get it? Where is she and why does he have it?" He almost howled in distress.

Shaking in anger. He then abruptly turned and fled the room before they could follow him, ask him more about when, what and who he meant – he was gone.

"Who does the blood run at the castle?" Iden asked Justina in concern as his friend quickly fled for elsewhere. For something was amiss that they had to get to the bottom of.

"I have no idea…" For she truthfully did not. Justina thankfully did not know much about the scary ass castle. "How did Fess get hold of Barrens mates blood?" She spoke aloud to herself.

The room went silent. No body knew.

"He might be mistaken?" Elfina asked. Could he be?

"Defiently not. Your senses are just coming in my mate. He smelt what he smelt. His mate was in that fucking vial. Poor thing. My poor friend Barren…" Iden tried to explain.

"You don't think…she's dead?" An uneasy gasp left his mates lips.

"Well how else would her essence be in a vial? "Iden retorted.

Justina didn't want to think the worst like the others did. Going back into the fridge and sniffing a few of the bottles. "They smell different to each other. Different people I think."

She herself preferred fresh blood. The idea of taking it and storing it made her feel too much of a monster to do so.

"This is freaky. Can we get out of here Iden?" Elfina asked. She shuddered as the castle creaked disturbing the bats.

"Yes." He simply stated ducking his head from the swarm. But first finding a bag and filling it with the left-over vials. He would get to the bottom of why that day's events had come to pass.

And where his age-old friends mate had gone.

The three walked towards the exit.

"Take a different exit." Justina said as the three finally reached the main back door. The door next to where Rhys had given her the munching out of her life…

Almost blushing at the memory of it. Her pussy clenched also at the memory.

"Why?" Iden asked.

"I don't want to see... Fess. Dead or alive."

"Understandable."

Elfina gripped tightly to him as though she did not want to see the blonde one with her own eyes either.

"But why did he keep saying two mates? I know you can't, but he seemed so obsessed with the idea..." Iden gulped. A flicker of doubt evidently crossing his handsome but worn-out face.

Having ventured, hardly sleeping just to rescue his mates sister just to have rocks thrown at him.

"Oh that?" Elfina grinned. "I finally realised why he had collected a harem of women and was so worked out about getting me back..."

The three stood still by the door.

"Cos he is a sex obsessed slut." Flicking her blonde hair out of the way, Justina spat.

"Nope." Elfina smirked. "He`s gay."

Stunned silence. Not even a peep out of them.

Moments later -"Ok. Very funny." Justina rolled her eyes snarkily. "I don't believe that for a second."

Iden was not convinced either. "Yes my mate. It does seem unlikely considering all he has done as of late… he has always been more of a ladies man then a man's man."

"Well, it's true." His frustrated mate snapped. "We were busy arguing on earth as I was telling him how stupid he were being by taking me there, and an auburn-haired man, rather dishy if I must say, came over to us and interrupted. He asked if all was well. Fess knew he was talking directly to him, but his cold stone heart? It couldn't process the idea of it, so he thought instead that I had two mates. This human man did not even look at me once. He did not see me at all. My first experience with being invisible and I'm not sure that I liked it…"

The other two were too gobsmacked to take in the emotion behind Elfina's heart felt statement. They would all have bet their entire life savings on Fess being straight! But then maybe it was the reason why he wanted so badly to have women hanging off of his arm for all their world to see…

Cover.

He did not want others to know what he was, nor had he accepted the fact for himself yet.

"Wow." Justina said in disbelief. Having being offed only to be used as a beard, "But his poor mate is about to become mate less. That does not seem fair."

"Sounds like a him problem." Iden shrugged.

A voice spoke out.

One that made Justinas heart flip, "Indeed." Rhys rounded the corner where he had been secretly listening to every word they spoke in the corridor. His ears twitching from all the information that he had heard.

His arms too.

For he wanted to pull his mate now simply into his arms and fuck his spunk all over her – and hide her there where she belonged.

His invisible hate – now gone.

"How long you been there?" Justina blinked at the sudden intrusion.

"Not long. Maybe ten minutes or more…"

"Ten minutes! Why you!" she swatted her worser half on the arm and in response he pulled her close, nuzzling her neck. Kissing it until the other pair of mates looked slightly grossed out.

"I was resting from all the Fess stomping."

"So, he's gone?" Her hopes soared through to the sky.

"Hopefully so. You two can go now." Rhys held out a fire ball to his bedazzled brother and now shaking mate. His apparent new favourite form of torture.

"Can`t you be fucking nice for once?" Iden scolded his brother.

"Fuck no! Now out you go!" Shooing them both away.

"Why did Fess have Barren`s mates blood in his fridge? Explain this brother!" Iden said before leaving.

"No idea. Now fuck off before this becomes an over eighteen show!"

That made them go, and it was back to the two. Eying each other hungrily as though they had not eaten all week.

The other one the meal that they desired.

"Justina." A whisper in her ear that made her tingle all over although it should not. The vamp who she belonged to, belonged with was – bad. But somewhere she guessed there was a hint of good in her handsome mate.

Her man smelled so divine that she could almost lick the psycho up with her tongue and gobble him up.

"Rhys. Fuck me. Now!" She demanded. He did not wait even a milli second and thrust into her hard. She could feel the large cock that pressed into her heat through their clothes. She almost moaned as he then plunged his tongue deep into her mouth and their lips met in sync.

His muscley arms around her so that they could not be separated ever again.

Nor did she want them to be.

So, this was the mate bond that hummed between them! The one that made even calm vamps like Dorothy lose their partners head over it. Before she had found the Wednesday Addams look alike - odd. But now – Justina knew why she had killed her own chosen mate.

For she would do the same if anyone got in the way of her and Rhys.

Her man. The only one for her. The only one she would ever love, could possibly love. Could ever need.

The evil one. Who was not as evil as she had so feared…

CHAPTER ELEVEN

Her man was getting impatient, "Get to my quarters! Now. Before I feast on you here again where all could see you cry tears of pleasure."

She pressed her thighs together as the heat rose.

"I don't know where they are. Damn creepy ass castle!" She moaned and pressed her lips back to his searching ones. Wanting to kiss him, to feel him but also wanting to stop so they could continue this elsewhere.

He pushed her into a wall. Kissing her. Biting her.

"You love it." He stopped kissing her and his eyes searched hers for an answer.

"I don't. I really don't."

"Well, we will have to do something about that. But first... first calls for the mating bond." He ignored her squeal picking her up almost dragging her kicking and screaming through the castle to his quarters where he was going to take her.

Not bothering with his crypt, for he wanted more room to fuck, frolic and feast...

Kicking the door to he placed her onto the large black settee and began slowly kissing her.

"Quickly!" she moaned. "I need you now!" No sooner had he said this then he had pushed her dress up and had his massive head right between her legs. Devouring her pussy again with his thick studded tongue, she almost screamed as he plunged it through her swollen lips, flicking her cunt gently.

Then lapping harder as the juices soon flowed from all the brazen muff eating.

It seemed she had a man with a slight pussy eating addiction. Or addicted to hers. For he had asked nothing else of her. As he ate and ate he played with her nipples making them hard like pebbles.

An invisible zing going from her heaving breasts right down to her crotch.

"I could die a happy vamp doing this!" He snarled hungrily. Preferring her cunt to the blood he loved so. Diving in again as though he had not eaten in weeks.

"Fuck you my monster. I'm going to come!" She howled as her pleasure peaked and her inner walls contracted around his fierce tongue. Feeling the hard cool metal of his stud touch her most sensitive parts.

She was glad Fess had killed her. Made her a vamp. For if not she would have had no one and him someone else…

She would die again, die every day. Become a vamp over and over, just to be with him.

"I`m your monster, and yours alone." He hissed as he bathed in her juices. Only stopping when she had finished screaming and twitching and spraying all over his hardened face.

She slowly pushed him away and put her thighs together as her nether regions became too sensitive. Having not had any knickers on from before when he had stuffed them in her mouth and then taken them away.

Kept them.

"Now what?" She asked still so full of need. She had not yet seen his cock, but she sure as hell wanted to! She had felt it more than once as he pressed into her.

"Now – this." His eyes darkened and dark magic filled his palms.

"You, you said you wouldn't use magic on me!" She trembled as she eyed the ball that had her name firmly on it.

"Never!" He almost spat. "I said I wouldn't use it on you. This is for something else; I promise you will enjoy it. Trust me? If not then I will put it out."

She remained unsure, "Not really...But go ahead..."

Trying to trust this man. Half of her did, just not her mind...

The ball of magic then became chains. She was chained to a bloody bed that had materialised, at the middle! She gasped as a diamond choker appeared around her neck in obvious ownership and a chain ran from it to his gripping hand.

"What the fuck!" She hollered and wriggled to get free on the bed. Trying to break the chains.

Hopeless.

She slapped him. Hard.

He simply laughed and clawed her dress off until she was laying there butt naked before her. He got up towering over her. Holding the chain in one hand he undressed himself with the other.

"Holy moly!" She gasped as his large cock swung free from his tight trousers. It was huge! She was surprised that it fit in the castle.

How the hell would he fit it in her she had no idea!

"That is not going to fit!" She gasped half in shock but also half in admiration at his beautiful appendage.

Rhys smirked, "Oh, it will my precious. Just needs a lot of lubricant." He started to stroke it as she eyed the monster cock eagerly.

Licking her lips. Craving it in the same way she craved cake.

"Oh, so you have some?" Justina asked with relief lining her beautiful face. Thank god!

"Oh no. That's where you come in my blonde beauty." He sniggered as he came over with his now large, erect cock hanging free over her face.

"Suck it." He said. "That is all the lube we need."

She was beginning to think again that her mate might be slightly evil. "What if I don't want to?" She said nervously but licking her lips, wondering what the cock would taste like if she ran her tongue up the also studded tip.

Likely heaven itself.

"Oh, you do." He grinned as he once again neared, this time nudging her lips open with his meaty goods.

She opened her mouth like a slut and swallowed the cock whole. Or what she could fit in! He gently at first thrusted in and out, in and out until it became faster. She gagged whilst chained to the bed. Unable to move away very far, but to be honest - not really wanting to.

This man, this cock that he wielded could possibly be the death of her. But she didn't care. Her parents would never know if that was how she ended…

They thought she had died anyway.

His desire for his mate, the one sucking his fierce cock became all the more shown, as it was not long before he groaned wickedly and with no prior warning sprayed his magnificent seed all over her face.

"Fuuuuuuck!" He roared as the cum poured down his stunning mates throat. He pulled back as he didn't want to be the death of her.

Quite yet.

He mustn't. He wouldn't…

Releasing his cock from its second home he pushed the hair out of his Justina's eyes, gazing into them as though she was all that.

He stroked her gorgeous face. "And you say I'm the wicked one! With your tongue greedily lapping at my thick cock, was it not you that was the wicked one just then my Justina?"

His words zinged to her crotch.

"Maybe." She grinned panting.

Pulling him in again for a lingering kiss that never seemed to end. He devoured her in the same way as she devoured him. And it was not long before she felt the magnificent cock that he owned breaking into her hidden place as he laid over her.

Dominating.

Having already hardened in seconds so that he could mate for the first time with his fated vampire mate.

Neither could wait...

"Shit!" She cried as she felt him fill her so very much that it almost hurt as he began thrusting with all his might. There was no going slow with this, he was determined to stake his claim on her.

Her eyes widened as he put his large palm over her mouth. Quieting her rising screams and loud moans. He whispered words of adoration as he pounded hard into her.

The sound of flesh slapping, pussy squelching.

She bit his hand gently and wriggled until he released his hand from her pretty mouth.

"Bite it properly, my dearest."

So, she did. And whilst he was shuddering his release again he bit into her own wrist with sharpened fangs. He collapsed on top of her being careful not to squash her with his massive, muscled weight.

After rolling onto his side, he allowed her to stick her fangs once again into his wrist. Where she fed.

"Its odd. But also, nice." She said drinking his purple blood as her eyes shone brightly as his lightening soul touched hers.

Rhys looked on the verge of coming hard again as she sucked with her fangs and lips, "Shut up! Devour my essence, make me yours!" He roared.

"You already are."

She noticed the way he now lit up now from his head to his toes. His masculine so rugged face so full of hidden joy at being hers, that he could not keep his joy contained any longer.

"As are you." Nibbling her petite wrist as he made his mark softly then roughly. Then going straight for the neck to taste more of her. The feeling of bliss that ran through them both as they drunk each other's life

173

essence. Drinking until they were almost devoured in every way possible.

They both passed out. His dark magic, the swirls releasing, as he did so. The castle rumbled as it changed. The two vamps were soon to arise again, bonded now as only life mates.

A vampire dark master and his new queen...

EPILOGUE 1

Two weeks later

Justina was now living full time at the humungous castle. No longer caring that she had to leave her clan for good after ten years to come there.

For she had a new one. Her mate. The boss of it and she, would run it together.

She smiled lovingly at the hulking hunk beside her in bed, snoring softly. A frown marred him even while he dreamed.

She could only guess what a beast like him would dream of!

Soon he would be waking – all of him. And he would openly not get up in the morning to conquer his part of the kingdom until he had stuffed one of her holes with his cock each and every morning.

For ownership, he had said with a possessive growl to her once.

But she knew that it was because he wanted to feel her. All of her. In the same way she felt him.

When he had tried her virgin bum for the first time they had required so much lube! If not she would not have been able to sit down for a long while…

The bond had thankfully worked even though she had already died long before it was created. As the bond then took, her lightness was the one that brought his dark magic down. And his magnificent but creepy castle became as it once were.

Beautiful. Normal.

The darkness was still there. But half the darkness part of the realm was back to the light. He still had magic. But it could not be used for badness no more. But surprisingly he was ok with that.

"Morning." She realised he was watching her intently. She could not believe how much he adored her so very much. Everything she wanted, everything she desired was now hers.

And he would fight for her along the way…

"Take your pjs off." He ordered. "I am going to breed you!" Ripping her night clothes off in an instant, kissing her open lips whilst he tried to spread her thighs open with his knees. Growling as his pre cum dripped.

She happily let him.

Opening her legs wide for her man to take her again.

But he could not breed her even if he wanted to. For she had discovered the day before that she may be the only vamp that could actually get pregnant.

For she was. She did not know how this would play out, only that when the magic left her mate, her master, – his seed planted in her and took hold in her womb.

So now Justina were pregnant with a monsters baby. She hadn't told him yet, not knowing how he would take it when she did.

Would he even want to be a father? He had love in his cold stone heart – you just had to dig deep to find it. She herself was ecstatic. From feeling weird, sicky, not the usual things that vamps felt and so deciding to secretly fly down and take a test.

Thinking it was nigh on impossible.

As she had stood shaking in the pharmacy toilet after hours.

Positive. Almost difficult to believe, but a joy none the less. A joy that she would take.

So now they were living in a castle of the light with a baby vamp on the way. Cedrik her horse also joining them soon much to her delight. A stable mate for Rhys`s crazy black unicorn with beady ass eyes that creeped her out.

The darkness that most had feared simply brought down by – love.

EPILOGUE 2

A few weeks prior.

In a craze Barren flew to the other side of the city. The past few mere hours he had been manically flying around, only stopping to do soul calls whilst looking for her so desperately that he could cry.

His fated mate. The one whose blood he had accidentally consumed back in that hell hole castle. Wondering now what had happened to her? Was she even alive? If she wasn't then he knew that he would never get over it.

Ever.

He had followed a fresh trail of her scent. The one that smelled so fucking fantastic, but now... but now the trail ran cold.

Suddenly he heard the sound of wings and a light crash. He looked over – Fess.

"What the fuck are you doing alive!" He yelled as he saw the guy tumble. Watching the blonde who was in a ball on the floor. Crumpled. Badly burnt. Only his face seemed unaffected by the fire that had been thrown at him.

But he were alive.

Fess let out a strangled cry, holding out his hands in a silent plea.

"Help me! Please!" He begged as his eyes found Barren`s crimson ones.

For no one else would see him. Now he was burnt over most of his body and invisible. He could die here, and no one would know.

Or care.

Barren angrily paced over to the other male. Knuckles clenching in sheer anger. Cracking them. Wanting to put the blonde one out of his fucking misery with his fists over and over. Instead, he touched his badly burned body – and shook him hard.

"Where did you get the blood in your fridge?" He yelled.

"The blood?" Fess frowned. What blood?

"The blood in your fucking fridge at the castle! It was her! My mate! I drank my own fucking mate!"

"Impossible."

"That it is not. I know what I tasted. I know what I drank…" Barren gritted his teeth. The dark-haired male still stood over the crumpled fair one. If he didn't need to know what happened to her then he would have killed the fucker!

He had grown up in a well too do neighbourhood it wasn't the way of his people to participate in mindless violence. Especially over someone who was as low as they could go. Fess certainly were.

But now he was a vamp and if anyone got in his way then he would start to act like one.

Having always preferred being down on earth then up there in the realms. Having wanted to clutch hold of his humanity just a bit longer. It was why he got on well with Ruby.

She was still getting used to being a non-human. He still wished he were one. Being mated to a human would now be as close as he could get to being one again.

Noone would take that away. He wouldn't let them. He would burn the fucker again!

"Rhys is trying to change for Justina. You will never change. You will always be scum!" Barren fumed.

"I'm scum? You have no idea mate. Rhys turned the teens into vamps to wind his brother up. He also has a farm down on earth. Why do you think he had so much stuff back at the castle? I know where it is, but I will not say. For he will kill me if I do. For he almost succeeded. Your mate, she must be at the farm."

"The farm?" Barrens stomach dropped.

"Yes. The farm. It's a people farm. A fresh blood farm."

Noone heard Barrens broken heart shatter into a million pieces. But now it had...

The end.

Thank you.

Printed in Great Britain
by Amazon

39856935R00108